Australian Museum

Guide to the Contents of the Australian Museum

Australian Museum

Guide to the Contents of the Australian Museum

ISBN/EAN: 9783337313302

Printed in Europe, USA, Canada, Australia, Japan

Cover: Foto ©Andreas Hilbeck / pixelio.de

More available books at **www.hansebooks.com**

GUIDE

TO THE CONTENTS

OF THE

AUSTRALIAN MUSEUM.

PRINTED BY ORDER OF THE TRUSTEES.

SYDNEY.

1890.

NOTE.

This Guide has been prepared and edited at the request of the Trustees, by the Secretary, Mr. S. Sinclair, who is indebted to the members of the staff for valuable assistance in its compilation.

E. P. RAMSAY,
Curator.

CONTENTS.

GUIDE

AUSTRALIAN MUSEUM.

———⋅◦⋅———

I.

INTRODUCTION.

THE AUSTRALIAN MUSEUM was founded in the year 1836. It was originally connected with the Botanic Gardens, and was located in a room in Macquarie Street. It was managed by a Committee, which in 1837 consisted of ALEXANDER MACLEAY, ESQ., J. V. THOMPSON, ESQ., CAPT. P. P. KING, R.N., HON. E. D. THOMPSON, M.C., CHARLES STURT, ESQ., GEORGE MACLEAY, ESQ., with GEORGE BENNETT, ESQ., as Secretary. In the year 1837, also, the first catalogue of the exhibits was published. From this it appears that there were at that time in the Museum—43 Specimens of Mammals; 348 of Birds; 21 of Reptiles; 215 of Insects; 25 of Shells; 34 of Skulls; 63 of Fossils and Minerals; 55 of Native Implements, etc., 804 in all, besides some collections of Fossils not enumerated.

The Museum was soon afterwards removed to the Surveyor-General's Office in Bridge Street, where it remained till 1849, in which year it was again removed to its present site at the corner of William and College Streets. The building at this time consisted of one room with a gallery. It still exists as the " *Old Wing* " of the present Museum.

The affairs of the Museum continued to be managed by the Committee until 1853, when it was incorporated by Act of Parliament, under a Board of Trustees composed of twelve Official Trustees, one Trustee named by the Governor and called the Crown Trustee, and twelve Elective Trustees, who were : ARTHUR A'BECKETT, ESQ., GEORGE BENNETT, ESQ., REV. W. B. CLARKE, FRED. O. DARVALL, ESQ., CAPT. P. P. KING, R.N., REV. R. L. KING, WILLIAM MACARTHUR, ESQ., HON. W. S. MACLEAY, GEORGE MACLEAY, ESQ., JOHN SMITH, ESQ., M.D., REV. GEO. E. TURNER, and GEORGE WITT, ESQ., M.D.

The First Crown Trustee was the HON. W. K. PARKER ; who was succeeded by the HON. SIR E. DEAS-THOMPSON, in 1857 ; and the HON. SIR ALFRED STEPHEN in 1880.

The Hon. Secretaries to the Committee from 1836 to 1853 were—DR. BENNETT, REV. W. B. CLARKE, LIEUT. R. LYND, REV. G. E. TURNER, and DR. WITT.

The Secretaries to the Trustees have been—MR. G. F. ANGAS, 1853 ; MR. S. R. PITTARD (Curator and Secretary), 1860 ; MR. GERARD KREFFT (Curator and Secretary), 1860 ; MR. CHAS. ROBINSON, 1873 ; MR. E. W. PALMER, 1877 ; MR. C. R. BUCKLAND, 1879 ; MR. S. SINCLAIR, 1882.

The first Curator of the Museum was MR. W. S. WALL; he was succeeded by MR. S. R. PITTARD in 1859 ; MR. GERARD KREFFT in 1861 ; and DR. E. P. RAMSAY in 1874.

In 1869 a plan for a handsome structure to contain the Museum, the Free Public Library, and the Art Gallery, was prepared, but only a small part of the portion intended for the Museum has been erected, viz., the western end, at present the principal part of the Museum, facing College street. The interior of the building as it now stands consists of a series of five large halls on the ground floor, with extensions from the terminal halls at each end ; and on the upper floor, which is reached by a broad handsome staircase, of the same number of halls without any extension.

The collections are arranged to the best advantage in these halls, but it is not possible in the unfinished state of the building to have a thoroughly complete or systematic arrangement. The exhibits, which in 1837 numbered about 800, may now be counted by hundreds of thousands, and require for their display far more space than is at the disposal of the Trustees. In some classes only a temporary arrangement has been attempted, and allied specimens, for want of room in the cases, are occasionally found in different parts of the building, so that the visitor is requested to be forbearing until with more accommodation a proper arrangement can be made.

This Guide is intended to help visitors in their examination of the Museum. For the ordinary visitor, who comes from curiosity or for amusement, the chapter "General Arrangement of the Museum," with the help of the plan, will probably be sufficient ; for those who wish to study, so as to gain at least an elementary knowledge of the animal and mineral kingdoms, the succeeding chapters have been prepared somewhat on the lines of a hand book ; while, for students of special subjects, separate and very complete catalogues have been prepared by order of the Trustees. A list of these as far as published, will be found appended to this Guide.

II.

GENERAL ARRANGEMENT OF THE MUSEUM.

ON entering the Museum from College-street the visitor passes directly into the large Central Hall, from whence other parts of the building are approached by the grand staircase leading to the upper floor, and by passages between pillars leading on the left to the Australian, and on the right to the Osteological Halls, and through these to the Mineral and the Ethnological Departments.

The Entrance or Central Hall is a lofty room, with a mosaic floor, occupying the central portion of the new building. It is not devoted specially to any one subject, but contains various specimens of interest. In different places on the floor are skeletons and mounted skins of animals—among them, Antelopes and Deer, two species of Rhinoceros, a female specimen of the Wild Cattle of India, Zebras, and skeletons of the Camel and Giraffe, and, in cases, mounted specimens of the Gorilla from West Africa, and Orang Outang from Borneo.

The case immediately facing the entrance contains a collection of Foreign Snakes in spirits; including the American Boa Constrictor and the Indian Python, the Anaconda of South America, the deadly Indian Cobra di Capello, and others from various parts of the world. In a separate and smaller case is an articulated skeleton of an Indian Python, and in another part of the Hall are a few mounted skins of non-venomous snakes (Pythons and Boas).

On the large central table the most conspicuous objects are casts of the *Megatherium giganteum* of South America and of the tusks of *Elephas ganesa* of India, a description of which will be found in chapter XIV. Palæontology.

Passing northwards—that is to the left of the entrance—is the Australian Hall, where specimens of the animals peculiar to Australia are exhibited.

Beginning at the left is a series of Marsupials. The first cases contain the Kangaroos and the Wombats. The next contain the Wallabies, Wallaroos, and the smaller species of Kangaroos. In the centre case on the end wall are the Jerboa- and Rat-Kangaroos, the Perameles, the Bandicoots and their allies. The next case to these in the right hand corner has a group of Tasmanian Mammals, among which are specimens of the Tasmanian Devil *(Sarcophilus)* and Tiger *(Thylacinus)*. On a shelf in the same case are Native Cats, &c. The Opossums and Native Bears follow and occupy one side of the room. The Placentals or Non-Marsupial Mammals—including Rats and Mice, Bats, the Dingo, Seals, &c., are further round in the case between the Opossums and the door leading to the Geological Hall.

Having reached this stage the visitor is recommended to return to the north end of the Australian Hall and to examine the Fishes and Reptiles in the table cases.

The Australian Fishes are in three large cases in the centre of the Hall. One contains mounted specimens, the others principally fishes preserved in spirits. The two remaining cases in the end room contain the Australian Snakes, Lizards, and Batrachians.

Overhead is the skeleton of a Sperm Whale *(Physeter macro cephalus)* stranded at Wollongong in 1860. It is about seventy feet in length. There are many other skeletons of whales in the Museum, but for want of room they cannot at present all be exhibited.

Returning now to the door at which we had previously arrived, a short flight of steps leads down to the Geological Hall. This is the oldest part of the Museum, and is known as the "Old Wing." It is to be devoted entirely to the Departments of Geology and Palæontology, but at present is in a transition state. The collections of insects which were previously deposited here have been removed to the upper floor of the new wing, and placed in cases prepared for their reception. The Foreign Mammals, which will by and by find a more suitable resting place, are in the meantime deposited in the wall cases and in the gallery without any special arrangement.

The cases in the centre are devoted to specimens of alluvial gold, auriferous quartz, and other gold-bearing rocks ; the largest contains gold, models of nuggets, and precious stones. In the gallery is a series illustrating the geology of the earth, arranged in the order of the strata, and showing forms of life which existed in former ages.

Leaving the Geological Hall and returning towards the grand staircase the wall cases on the left hand contain a general collection of mounted fishes, and in the corner beside the staircase are cases containing the Palæichthyan Fishes, or Sharks, Rays, and Ganoids, which latter are the last survivors of the oldest created vertebrate animals ; among them is the curious mud fish of Queensland (Ceratodus forsteri). Other fishes will be found exhibited in cases on the Upper Floor temporarily arranged.

We have now returned to our starting point and, passing to the southwards, will visit the Osteological Halls. Here are exhibited Skeletons, both recent and fossil. Beginning at the left hand is a series of six aboriginal human skeletons. Beside them are the skeletons of a Gorilla, a Chimpanzee, and other monkeys Ranged on the wall behind the skeletons is a series of skulls, and among them is one disarticulated—that is with the bones separated and named for the use of students. Further on in the same case is a collection of casts of heads and faces, from life, of South Sea Islanders prepared by Dr. Otto Finsch of Bremen ; for particulars of which see chapter XVI., Anthropology and Ethnology.

Continuing along the same row of cases, and passing the pillars into the next room, we come to skeletons of the Carnivorous Mammalia,—Lions, Tigers, Wolves, Dogs, &c. Past the door leading to the Ethnological Hall and along the end wall are skeletons of the Bear, Pig, Horse, Zebra, Deer, and other orders of Mammalia which for want of space cannot be arranged in their natural sequence. The case at the side wall opposite the door contains skeletons of Kangaroos, Wombats and other typical Australian animals, including Whales and Seals, also a skeleton, with the different bones named, of the gigantic Cod-perch of our eastern coast ; at the corner beside the pillar are bones of the Moas, large extinct birds of New Zealand, with skeletons of an Ostrich and an Emu beside them for comparison ; and in the desk case between the pillars is a collection of bones of these and other gigantic New Zealand birds.

Passing round the pillar, are cases containing a further series of skeletons of Whales, Dolphins, Dugongs, Manatees, &c.

One of the most remarkable fossil skeletons is that of the great Irish Elk (*Megaceros hibernicus*) with its magnificent antlers. This splendid animal is now extinct but its bones are found embedded in the peat bogs of Ireland and elsewhere. This specimen is considered one of the largest and best preserved in any museum. Its antlers measure 9 feet from tip to tip.

Other large skeletons are those of a Hippopotamus, a Rhinoceros, an Elephant, a Crocodile from Queensland, a Camel, and a Giraffe.

A glass case in the centre of the Hall contains skeletons of cartilaginous Fishes—Sharks, and Rays. These are exceedingly difficult to prepare and are very seldom to be seen in any museum.

The skeletons of Birds will also be found in a separate table case.

In the end room are four desk cases devoted to the fossil remains of extinct Australian animals; among which are specially to be noticed the skull and bones of the *Nototherium* and *Diprotodon*, extinct gigantic Marsupials allied to the Wombat and Native Bear, and teeth of the curious *Sceparnodon* (Ramsay). These fossils prove that there existed in olden times very large Kangaroos and other marsupials, compared with which the largest of the modern Kangaroos would be small, and there have also apparently been large carnivorous or flesh-eating marsupials which have been called *Thylacoleo* or Marsupial Lions.

The door opening off this room leads to the new annexe which is devoted to Ethnology and is called the Ethnological Hall. It is of so much interest that to attempt a description of it in the limits of this chapter would be useless, and the visitor is requested to turn at once to chapter XVI., Anthropology and Ethnology.

Returning again to the centre of the building it is time to ascend to the upper floor and examine the treasures stored there.

We first enter a lofty hall and our attention is at once attracted by the mounted examples of large Sunfishes *(Orthagoriscus mola)*, Sharks, Rays, Swordfishes, Dolphins, and Porpoises, hanging from the gallery; among others the ferocious White Pointer, Tiger and Hammerheaded Sharks; the Black Sting-Ray; and the curious Thresher, which uses its long tail with no little effect on the back of Whales. Most of these have been caught in Port Jackson and its vicinity. After looking at these we should observe also the Crocodiles, Tortoises, and other large animals mounted in groups.

In crossing the hall we pass the collections of Insects. These are at present placed in five cases running across the centre of the room. Two of these contain the type or index collections of Foreign *Coleoptera* (Beetles) and *Lepidoptera* (Butterflies and Moths) and the representative collections (Australian and Foreign) of *Orthoptera* (Grasshoppers, Locusts, &c.), *Diptera* (Flies, &c.), *Neuroptera* (Dragon-flies, &c.), *Rhynchota* (Bugs, &c.), and *Hymenoptera* (Bees, Wasps, &c.) The other cases contain the Australian collections of *Coleoptera* and *Lepidoptera*.

The next cases to demand our attention are those containing the collections of Shells. These are always attractive from their beautiful forms and colours. Shells are the homes of soft bodied animals—the Mollusca—and though it is impossible to understand their structure and life habits from a study of the shells alone, yet they are interesting as the skeletons of other animals are interesting, and they show even a greater variety of form. Combined with the general collection is the Hargraves' Collection, collected by Mr. Hargraves, from whom they were purchased by the late Mr. Thos. Walker of Yaralla, and presented to the Australian Museum. The specimens which belong to this collection are marked "Hargraves' Coll." This combined collection, which numbers many thousand species, is considered one of the largest in the world. As the arrangement of these is still in progress it will be impossible to say more at present with regard to their disposition. A Catalogue of the whole will be issued when the work is completed.

Beyond the cases containing shells is a room devoted at present to a portion of the Mineral Collection. If the visitor begins at the left-hand side, and follows the cases round, the labels will explain the specimens. It would not be easy to give an exact description here, as this department will be subject to frequent changes until it is removed to its permanent quarters in the old wing.

In the north wing of this floor is the collection of Australian Birds in which about 700 species are represented. A passing glance may be bestowed on a few of the most striking genera peculiar to Australia. Some of the most remarkable are to be found among the Bower-building birds (*Scenopœidœ*), including the Cat-birds, Regent-bird, and Satin-birds, which are noted for their peculiar habits of making playgrounds or bowers of sticks, and ornamenting them with feathers, bones, shells, berries and other attractive objects ; the Scrub-birds (*Atrichia*) with their truly wonderful powers of ventriloquism ; the Lyre-birds (*Menura*) noted for their great power of mimicry ; the many and varied species of Honey-eaters (*Meliphagidœ*) ; and the gorgeously plumaged Cockatoos, Parrots, and Lorikeets belonging to the family *Psittacidœ*. There are also the Mound-raising birds (*Megapodiidœ*) which deposit their eggs in large tumuli of decaying vegetable matter, and leave them to be hatched by the heat from the fermentation of the mass; this family includes the Wattled Talegallus or Brush Turkey (*Talegallus lathami*), the Ocellated Leipoa (*Leipoa ocellata*) better known to the colonists as the Mallee-hen, and the Mound-raising Megapode (*Megapodius tumulus*); the members of this last genus are not confined to Australia, but are also found on the adjacent islands, and in New Guinea. The family *Struthionidœ* is represented by the well known Emu, now being exterminated, and the Cassowary (*Casuarius australis*), a denizen of the dense and almost impenetrable scrubs of North-eastern Queensland, which is also rapidly becoming extinct. The peculiar Cape Barron Goose (*Cereopsis novæ-hollandiæ*) is worthy of attention, as it is the only species of the genus, and with the Semipalmated Goose (*Anseranas melanoleuca*), and the well-known Musk Duck (*Biziura lobata*), is confined to Australia. The Cereopsis, is allied to a fossil form (*Cnemiornis calcitrans*) found in the New Zealand Moa-beds. The Sea Birds are well represented, from the gigantic Albatross, with its wide expanse of wing, to the little Storm Petrel. Many of these are not peculiar to Australia, although some are only to be found in the southern seas. Fuller details of the Australian Birds will be found in Chapter VII.

In the south wing of this floor is the collection of Foreign Birds, which for want of sufficient space is not arranged strictly in order of families; a few of the most important genera will be found mentioned in Chapter VI. Special attention is drawn to the various groups of Paradise Birds and Trogons arranged in the pillar cases.

Beyond the Birds, at the north end of the building, are collections of Invertebrata—including the *Crustacea*, (Crabs); the *Arachnida*, (Spiders); the *Echinodermata*, (Star-fishes and Sea-urchins); the *Zoophytes*; and lower forms of life.

III.

GENERAL DIVISION OF THE ANIMAL KINGDOM.

THE Animal Kingdom is rather arbitrarily divided into two great Sub-kingdoms known as the Vertebrata and the Invertebrata.

The **VERTEBRATA** include all animals having a back-bone, which surrounds and protects a persistent cellular substance, called the "notochord or spinal marrow"; they have a bony skull and skeleton (except in the case of certain classes of fishes hereafter mentioned), and generally four limbs, which however in some cases are rudimentary. The vertebrated animals are divided into five classes, viz., Mammalia, Aves, Reptilia, Batrachia, and Pisces, which are again subdivided into orders as in the following tables.

Class I.—MAMMALIA.

Order	I.—Bimana	Two-handed animals—Men.
„	II.—Quadrumana	Four-handed animals—Monkeys and Lemurs.
„	III.—Carnivora	Flesh-eating animals—Lions, Tigers, Cats, Dogs, Bears, Seals, &c.
„	IV.—Insectivora	Insect-eating animals—Moles, Hedgehogs, &c.
„	V.—Chiroptera	Hand-winged Mammalia—Insectivorous and Fruit-eating Bats.
,	VI.—Rodentia	Gnawing animals — Rats, Rabbits, Squirrels, Porcupines, Beavers,&c.
„	VII.—Ungulata	Hoofed animals—Elephants, Rhinoceros, Horses, Pigs, Hippopotami, Camels, Oxen, Deer, Sheep, Goats.
„	VIII.—Cetacea	Aquatic animals—Whales.
„	IX.—Sirenia	„ „ —Dugongs & Manatees

Class I.—MAMMALIA—*continued:*

Order	X.—Edentata	Toothless animals—Sloths, Anteaters, &c.
,,	XI.—Marsupialia	Pouched animals—Kangaroos, Wombats, Opossums, &c.
,,	XII.—Monotremata	Oviparous or egg-laying Mammals—Platypus and Echidna.

Class II.—AVES.

Order	I.—Accipitres	Falcons, Vultures, Owls, &c.
,,	II.—Psittaci	Parrots, Cockatoos, &c.
,,	III.—Picariae	Swifts, Kingfishers, Cuckoos, &c.
,,	IV.—Passeres	Swallows, Crows, Birds of Paradise, Honeyeaters, Finches, Pittas, &c.
,	V.—Columbae	Pigeons.
,	VI.—Gallinae	Fowls, Pheasants, Megapodes.
,,	VII.—Grallatores	Plovers, Snipes, Herons, &c.
,,	VIII.—Natatores	Gulls, Ducks, Pelicans, &c.
,,	IX.—Struthiones,	Cassowaries, Apteryx, Ostriches, Emus.

Class III.—REPTILIA.

Order	I.—Chelonia	Tortoises and Turtles.
,,	II.—Crocodilia	Crocodiles and Alligators.
,,	III.—Lacertilia	Lizards.
,,	IV.—Ophidia	Snakes.

Class IV.—BATRACHIA.

Sub-Order	I.—Salientia	Frogs and Toads
,,	II.—Gradientia	Newts and Salamanders.
,,	III.—Apoda	Cœcilians.

Class V.—PISCES.

Sub-Class I.—PALÆICHTHYES.

Order	I.—Chondropterygii	Sharks, Rays and Chimæras.
,,	II.—Ganoidei	Plated Fishes

Class V.—PISCES—*continued:*

Sub-Class II.—TELEOSTEI.

Order	III.—Acanthopterygii	Perch, Mackerel, Mullet, &c,
,,	IV.—Pharyngognathi	Parrot-fishes, &c.
,,	V.—Anacanthini	Cod, Beardie, Sole, &c.
,,	VI.—Physostomi	Garfish, Salmon, Herring, &c.
,,	VII.—Lophobranchii	Sea Horses, Pipe fishes.
,,	VIII.—Plectognathi	Leather jackets, Toad fishes, &c.

Sub-Class III.—CYCLOSTOMATA.

,,	IX.—Petromyzontidæ	Lampreys.

Sub-Class IV.—LEPTOCARDII.

,,	X.—Cirrostomi	Lancelets.

The **INVERTEBRATA**— the second grand division of the Animal Kingdom—include generally all those forms of animals which do not possess a backbone. There is, however, such a great variety in this division that they have been classified into the following sub-kingdoms.

Sub-Kingdom I.—MOLLUSCA.

Class I.—CEPHALOPODA.

Sub-Class I.—DIBRANCHIATA.

Order	1.—Octopoda	Octopus or Poulpe and Argonaut.
,,	2.—Decapoda	Squids and Cuttlefishes.

Sub-Class II.—TETRABRANCHIATA

Order	—Nautilidæ	Pearly Nautilus.

Class II.—PTEROPODA.

Order	1.—Thecosomata	Cavolina, Hyalea, &c.
,,	2.—Gymnosomata	Clio.

Class III.—GASTROPODA.

Sub-Class I.—PROSOBRANCHIATA.

Order	1.—Pectinibranchiata	Rock-snails, Whelks, Olives, Harp-shells, Cones, Strombs or Wing shells, &c.
,,	2.—Scutibranchiata	Nerites, Top-shells, Ear-shells and Limpets.
,,	3.—Polyplacophora	Chitons.

Sub-Kingdom I.—MOLLUSCA—*continued:*

Sub-Class II.—OPISTOBRANCHIATA.

ORDER　1.—Tectibranchiata　Bubble Shells, Sea Hares, Umbrella-shells.

,,　　2.—Nudibranchiata　Sea Lemons (*Doris*), &c.

Sub-Class III.—NUCLEOBRANCHIATA or Heteropoda.
Firola, Carinaria, Atlanta.

Sub-Class IV.—PULMONATA.

ORDER　1.—Stylommatophora　Slugs, Snails.

,,　　2.—Basommatophora　Water-snails, False Limpets.

Class IV.—SCAPHOPODA　　Tooth-shells (*Dentalium*).

Class V.—PELECYPODA or LAMELLIBRANCHIATA.

ORDER　1.—Siphonida　Clam-shells (*Tridacna*) Cockles, Tellens,　Wedge-shells, Gapers, Razor-shells, Watering pot-shells, Burrowing-shells, &c., &c.

,,　　2.—Asiphonida　Oysters, Scallops, Pearl-oysters Mussels, Arks, Trigonia, River-mussels (*Unio*), &c.

Class VI.—MOLLUSCOIDEA.

ORDER　1.—Tunicata　Sea-squirts, Cungeeboys,—Ascidians, Salpae.

,,　　2.—Brachiopoda　Lamp-shells,　Terebratula, Waldheimia, Kraussiana, Spirifer.

,,　　3.—Polyzoa　Sea-mats, — Flustra, Catenicella, Lepralia, Membranipora, Retepora.

Sub-Kingdom II.—ARTHROPODA.

Class I.—INSECTA.

Family 1.—COLEOPTERA	Beetles.
2.—HYMENOPTERA	Bees, Wasps, Ants, &c.
3.—NEUROPTERA	Dragon-flies, May-flies, &c.
4.—LEPIDOPTERA	Moths, Butterflies, &c.
5.—DIPTERA	Flies.
6.—APHANIPTERA	Fleas.
7.—RHYNCHOTA	Plant Bugs, Water Bugs, &c.
8.—ORTHOPTERA	Grasshoppers,　Locusts, Crickets, Cockroaches, &c.
9.—THYSANURA	Silver-fish or Lepisma, &c.

Sub-Kingdom II.—ARTHROPODA—*continued:*

Class II.—MYRIAPODA	Centipedes, Millipedes, Forty-legs (*Cermatio*).
Class III.—ARACHNIDA	Spiders, Scorpions.
Class IV.—CRUSTACEA	Crabs, Lobsters, Prawns.

Sub-Kingdom III.—VERMES.

Worms, Rotifers, Serpulæ, Sea Mice, Earthworms, Leeches, Tapeworms.

Sub-Kingdom IV.—ECHINODERMATA.

Feather-stars, Star-fish, Sand or Brittle-stars, Sea-eggs, Sea-cucumbers (Trepang.)

Sub-Kingdom V.—COELENTERATA.

Class I.—SCYPHOMEDUSAE	Jelly-fish.
Class II.—SIPHONOPHORA	Portuguese man-of-war.
Class III.—HYDROMEDUSAE	Zoophytes—Sea Firs, Sertularia, Tubularia, Millepora.
Class IV.—ZOANTHARIA	Sea Anemones, Reef-building Corals.
Class V.—ALCYONARIA	Gorgonia, Red Coral.
Class VI.—PORIFERA	Sponges.

Sub-Kingdom VI.—PROTOZOA.

Infusoria, Foraminifera, Amoeba.

IV.

MAMMALIA.

Class I.—Mammalia.—These are warm-blooded animals, having a heart with four cavities, and a complete double circulation; possessed of two pairs of well developed limbs (except in certain marine forms), which may be greatly modified to suit individual requirements; having the lungs completely separated from the abdomen; the skin more or less clothed with hair; and in the female producing living young (except in Echidna and Ornithorhynchus, see pages 49 and 50), which are nourished for some time after birth,—hence the name Mammalia, from the Latin *Mamma*, a breast. Mammalia are divided into Orders as shown on page 15.

Order I.—BIMANA, or two-handed animals, is confined to Human Beings. The history and structure of the different races of men inhabiting the world are illustrated in the Museum by skeletons, casts, and Ethnological specimens, which are referred to more fully in chapters XIII. Osteology and XVI. Anthropology and Ethnology.

The human skeleton may be taken as a type of other mammalian skeletons, and of most other vertebrates. The four limbs are present in all the Mammalia, whether we call them hands, feet, wings, fins, or flippers; the backbone is found in all, and so is a skull to enclose the brain.

The human race is generally recognised to be essentially one, but it is divided in a most complex manner into varieties and groups which cross and recross one another.

Order II.—QUADRUMANA, or four-handed animals, includes Monkeys and Lemurs. Their teeth are generally the same as in man, but not always so regular. The thumbs on both fore and hind limbs can be used as in man's hands—but sometimes the thumbs are wanting.

Following modern scientific usage the name *Quadrumana* is not correct, as the monkeys have really *two hands* and *two feet*, and in other respects they are so similar in structure to men that the *Bimana* and *Quadrumana* are now placed in one order and called *Primates*. But for convenience the older classification is here retained, as being more generally understood.

The **MONKEYS** are represented in the Museum by the Anthropoid, or manlike Apes—viz. the Gorilla, the Orang-Outang, the Chimpanzee, the Gibbon, and by other Monkeys less like man.

The **Gorilla** (*Troglodytes gorilla*) is represented by specimens in a case between the pillars at the north side of the Central Hall and by a skeleton in the Osteological collection. It is the most manlike of the Monkeys, but its ferocious appearance shows it to be far below even the lowest men. It is a native of Western Africa. Many tales are told of its daring and its encounters with travellers in the African forests. The ordinary height of the Gorilla is about five feet six inches. The jaws are of tremendous weight and power. The huge eye-teeth or canines of the male, which are fully exhibited when, in his rage, he draws back his lips and shows the red colour of the inside of his mouth, lend additional ferocity to his aspect. The arms are very long and powerful, extending nearly as low as the knees. The legs are short and decrease in size from below the knee to the ankle, having no calf. The great length of the arms and the shortness of the legs form two of the chief differences between it and man. From the structure of its skeleton, the Gorilla is not adapted for the erect posture ; its favorite attitude is semi-erect with the weight partly resting on the knuckles of its long arms, and in this way it swings itself along as with a pair of crutches. It has been seen, however, to walk with its hands clasped across the back of its head and when enraged it is said to stand erect beating its chest with its hands.

The **Chimpanzee** (*Troglodytes niger*) is also a native of Africa. It is a much less formidable animal than the Gorilla, although it is quite able to defend itself against its foes in the forest. A specimen is to be seen in one of the cases in the gallery of the "Old Wing."

c

The **Orang-Outangs** (*Simia satyrus* and *S. morio*) are in a case near the Gorilla, in the Australian Hall. These Monkeys are natives of Borneo and Sumatra. They live in the trees and progress by climbing among the branches from tree to tree. "The Orangs all have ruddy-brown hair, the tinge being decidedly red, a dark face, with small eyes, small nose and great projecting jaws. What strikes one directly, on looking at a well-mounted specimen, is the great length of the fore-limbs, which reach far towards the ankle, the length of the muzzle and the extraordinary breadth of the face under the eyes, where the flatness resembles a mask more than a natural growth. In the females and young this growth of the cheek-bone and its covering of fat and skin are not seen; and it appears to be a mark of male beauty, as are also two sets of ridges on the skull which greatly resemble those of the Gorilla."

The **Gibbon** (*Hylobates leuciscus*) also from Southern Asia and the Malay Archipelago, is in the Gallery of the "Old Wing." It is remarkable for its fore-limbs being so long as almost to reach the ground when the animal stands erect.

Other Monkeys are exhibited in cases in the "Old Wing." The principal specimens are—

Sacred Apes (*Semnopitheci*) from India and Java and one from Tonga, South Seas (*S. obscurus*) distinguished by their slender forms, round heads, long tails, and by the fore limbs being much shorter than the hind limbs, and the thumbs small, sometimes almost rudimentary.

The Colobi, allied to the last, but natives of Africa.

The Patas—(*Cercopithecus* or *Chlorocebus ruber*) and

The Moustache Monkey (*Cercopithecus cephus*) from Western Africa, which have cheek pouches large enough to stow away a supply of food.

The Red Teetee—(*Callithrix ruber*) and several representatives of the Macaque family from India and the Eastern Archipelago. One species of this Monkey is to be found on the Rock of Gibraltar and on the opposite coast of Africa.

The Egyptian Sacred Ape.

The Baboon—(*Cynocephalus babouin*) and **Mandrill** (*Mormon maimon* or *Papio mormon*) from Africa and Arabia. These have the fore and hind limbs of nearly equal length, and have very powerful jaws.

The Monkeys of America are distinguished from those of the Old World by their having broad noses and widely separated nostrils. They are all of small size, and are mostly natives of Brazil. They are represented by:—

> **The Howling Monkeys** *(Mycetes seniculus)*, the males of which have a most extraordinary cry.

> **The Spider Monkeys** *(Ateles)*, with long slender limbs.

> **The Marmoset** *(Hapale jacchus)*, and the **Pigmy Marmoset** *(H. pygmæa)*, which are great favourites, being of grotesque appearance and easily tamed.

The LEMURS form the lowest family of Quadrumana. They have very long hind limbs, and bushy tails. They habitually use all four feet in locomotion like the lower groups of Monkeys, They are agile climbers, and are able to grasp firmly with the hind foot, but the tail· is not usually prehensile. The form of the skull and the simpler structure of the brain indicate a lower grade than the Monkeys. A remarkable peculiarity is the presence of a fringe or frill situated on the floor of the mouth in front of the tongue. The head-quarters of the Lemurs is the island of Madagascar; but members of the family are to be found also on the continent of Africa and in some of the islands of the East-Indian Archipelago. Some species chiefly subsist on fruits, but many are insect-eating and others prey upon small birds and eggs. The largest is only about three feet high (*Indris*). The most remarkable is the Aye Aye (*Chiromys madagascariensis*) from Madagascar. The middle finger of its fore-foot is long and slender, and is used for extracting worms and caterpillars from their holes in the branches of trees, and its front teeth are very sharp for gnawing the stems of plants. Other specimens are the Black-faced Lemur and the Anguan Lemur from Madagascar; and *Galago demidoffi* and *G. galleni* from Africa.

Order III.—CARNIVORA.—This order comprises the flesh-eating animals, or beasts of prey. It includes Lions, Tigers, Cats, Dogs, &c., on the land, and Seals, Walruses, &c., in the water. They have well developed teeth, and four or more claws on each foot.

The FELIDÆ, or Cat family, comprises Lions, Tigers, Cats, &c., and is the most highly developed of the Carnivora. These animals have short jaws and rounded heads, and generally four toes visible on the hind, and five on the front feet. They have powerful limbs, and spring on their prey. Their claws are retractile or capable of being drawn back when not in use. They walk on their toes, and the heel does not touch the ground—hence they are called digitigrade. They are to be found all over the world, except in Madagascar and Australia. This family is represented in the Museum by the following specimens :—

The Lion—(*Felis leo*) found throughout Africa and South-western Asia.

The Tiger—(*Felis tigris*) found in almost all countries of Asia. It is a more dangerous animal than the Lion, and is remarkable for the beautiful stripes on its body.

The Leopard—(*Felis pardus*) a native of Africa, and Asia, extending its range to Japan and Saghalien.

The Puma—(*Felis concolor*) of America ; a powerful, but rather cowardly animal, seldom known to attack man.

The Cats—Nubian Cat ; Java Cat ; Pampas Cat ; Wild Cat of Europe and Northern Asia ; Spotted American Cat ; Common Domestic Cat. The Nubian Cat is supposed to be the ancestor of the Domestic Cat.

The Lynx—(*Felis lynx*) closely allied to the cat, but with a shorter tail.

The Spotted Hyæna—(*Hyæna crocuta*) from South Africa.

The Civet Cat—(*Viverra zibetha*) from Ceylon, (*V. civetta*) from South Africa, (*V. indica*) from India.

The Genette—(*Genetta tigrina*) from South Africa, which resembles a cat.

The Ichneumons—(*Herpestes paludinosus*) from South Africa and (*H. javanicus*), which are sometimes tamed and used to keep down snakes, lizards, etc.

The Mongoose—(*Herpestes griseus*) from India.

The CANIDÆ, or Dog family, comprises Dogs, Wolves, Foxes and Jackals. Like the *Felidæ*, they are digitigrade, or walk on their toes, and have four toes visible on the hind, and five on the front feet ; they do not, however, spring on their prey in the same stealthy manner, but rather run it down. They differ from the Cats in having non-retractile claws and the fore part of the skull elongated. They are represented by the following specimens :—

The Dog—(*Canis familiaris*). The Blood Hound ; the Terrier; the Poodle. It is uncertain from what wild species the dog has descended. It is only known now in the domestic state, and such wild dogs as exist are evidently offshoots from some domestic dog. The dogs of different countries show a remarkable resemblance to the wild species found in the same countries. The different varieties of dogs will interbreed, and will do so even with the wolf and the jackal.

The Wolf—(*Canis lupus*) found all over Europe, Asia, and North America.

The Jackal—*(Canis aureus* and *C. mesomelas)* from India and South Africa.

The Foxes—(*Vulpes*) differ somewhat from the other *Canidæ* They are found in both the old and new worlds. Specimens exhibited are :—The Common Fox—(*Vulpes vulgaris*); the Arctic Fox (*V. lagopus*) from the Arctic regions of both hemispheres, one variety of which is of a blue colour all the year round, and another is of a brown colour in summer and changes to white in winter ; the Red Fox of Canada (*V. fulvus*) ; and others.

The MUSTELIDÆ, or Weasel family, includes a number of, small, long-bodied, but short-legged Carnivora. Many of them have the power of ejecting a most disagreeable odour, by means of a secretion from a specially developed gland. The following species of this family are exhibited :—

The Marten, (*Martes abietum*) from Great Britain.

The Common Weasel—(*Mustela vulgaris*).

The Japanese Weasel—(*Mustela itatsi*).

The Polecat—(*Mustela putorius*).

The Ferret—(*Mustela furo*).

The Stoat or Ermine—(*Mustela erminea*) famed for its fur.

The Minx (*Mustela vison*) from North America.

The Chorok—(*Mustela siberica*).

The Skunk—(*Mephitis mephitica*) which has the most powerful odour of all Mustelidæ. No amount of washing will remove it from one's clothes if it once touches them.

The Badger—(*Meles taxus*) of Europe.

The Otters—(*Lutra vulgaris*) and (*L. chinensis*) or Chinese Otter, which are nearly allied to the Weasels. They have webbed feet, and live in holes in the banks of rivers and lakes. One species (not yet represented in the collection) is a sea otter, and is found on the coasts of the North Pacific.

The URSIDÆ, or Bear family, is distinguished from the foregoing by walking on the soles of the foot; it is, therefore, called plantigrade. The Bears have long fur, straight claws, short tails, and are generally large heavily-built animals. They are not solely carnivorous, most species using vegetable food. They are found in Europe, Asia, and America; but are not known in South Africa or Australia. The following specimens are shewn :—

The Polar Bear—(*Ursus* or *Thalassarctos maritimus*). This is the largest of the Bears. It inhabits the Arctic Ocean, and lives on fish, seals, etc. It is a good swimmer.

The Grizzly Bear—(*Ursus ferox*). An inhabitant of Western North America, and the most dangerous wild animal of that continent. Fossil remains show that at one time it was found in Europe.

The Brown Bear—(*Ursus arctos*). The Bear of Northern Russia and Siberia. This is the species that until recent times was found in Great Britain.

The Racoons—(*Procyon*) are small animals very closely allied to the Bears. They belong exclusively to America, but species resembling them are found in other parts of the world.

The PINNIPEDIA, or Seal family, differs very materially from all land carnivora. It consists, however, of flesh eating, air breathing mammals fitted for an aquatic life. These have close warm fur, short tails, and flippers instead of feet. In the water their locomotion is rapid and graceful, on shore it is laborious and awkward. They range over all seas, and are often found far from land, but always come to the shore at the breeding season. The best known species are :—

The Earless Seals—(*Phocidæ*) found in nearly all seas of the Northern Hemisphere, and even in the inland Caspian Sea, and a few in the Southern ocean. They sometimes reach a length of ten feet. Their fur is short and close.

The Eared Seals —(*Otariidæ*) have small external ears, and a beautiful soft under-fur. They are better able to get about on land than the *Phocidæ*. The Seals found on the coast of N.S.W. are (*Arctocephalus cinereus,* and (*Stenorhynchus leptonyx*) the former is a Fur or Eared Seal ; the latter commonly called the Sea Leopard, is one of the *Phocidæ*. Specimens are shown in the Upper Floor, Central Hall.

The Walrus—(*Trichechidæ*) of which there are two species, are distinguished by their immense canine teeth, which project downwards like tusks to a length of twenty inches or more. Skulls of both species are exhibited in the Osteological collection.

Order IV—INSECTIVORA.—This order comprises a number of small animals, such as Moles, Shrews, and Hedgehogs,

which feed on insects and worms. They are found in all parts of the world, except Australia and South America. The molars of animals of this order are sharp serrated teeth, but the teeth vary considerably in the different genera. They are nearly all nocturnal animals, that is they come out by night to search for food and sleep by day ; and some of them hybernate, or remain dormant during the winter months.

The MOLES (*Talpidæ*) are formed for burrowing in the earth. They have short powerful claws, very small eyes, and beautifully soft fur, which will lie either way, and offers no impediment to the animal's progress through its tunnels. But one group of Moles (*Myogale*) has its feet and tail modified so as to fit it for an aquatic life. They are represented by :—

The Common Mole—(*Talpa europœa*) of Europe.

The Water Mole—(*Myogale pyrenaica*) from the Pyrenees.

The Golden Mole—(*Chrysochloris capensis* and *C. villosa*) from the Cape of Good Hope.

THE SHREWS (*Soricidæ*) are little animals very like mice in outward appearance.

THE HEDGEHOGS—(*Erinaceidæ*) are well known by their spines, and their habit of rolling themselves into a ball for defence purposes when frightened.

The Common Hedgehog—(*Erinaceus europœus*) is a native of Great Britain and other parts of Europe.

Order V.—CHIROPTERA.—This order comprises the Bats, which are distinguished by their adaptability for flight. The fore limbs and fingers are enormously elongated; and a membrane, which is a continuation of the skin of the body, stretched over them forms the wings. The hind limbs are short, but have large hooked claws by which the animals hang, head downwards, in the trees when at rest. The Bats are mostly crepuscular in their habits, that is they sleep by day and come out to search for food in the twilight, and many of them hybernate. They are found in all parts of the world. There are two suborders—the Insect-eating, and the Fruit-eating.

The INSECT-EATING BATS are very common, and typical species of foreign genera are :—

The **Great Bat**—(*Megaderma*) of Asia and Africa.

The **Large Bat**—(*Vesperugo noctula*) of England.

The **White Bat**—(*Diclidurus albus*) of South America.

The **Vampire**—(*Vampyrus*) of America.

The **Blood-Sucking Bat**—(*Desmodus*) of America.

A number of specimens will be seen also in the Australian collection.

The FRUIT-EATING BATS, known in Australia as Flying Foxes, attain a great size. The largest of these Bats (*Pteropus*) has often four or five feet expanse of wing, while the smallest (*Macroglossus minimus*) is about the size of a large mouse. Typical specimens shewn are :—

Pteropus poliocephalus of Australia.

Pteropus jubatus of the Phillipine Islands.

Pteropus grandis of the Solomon Islands.

Pteropus alboscapulatus of the Duke of York Islands.

Macroglossus minimus of New Guinea and Australia.

Harpyia macrocephalus, var. of New Guinea and New Britain.

Order VI.—RODENTIA.—This is one of the largest orders among the Mammalia both in the numbers of its genera and species, although the animals themselves composing it are usually of small size. It includes the Rats, Mice, Rabbits, Squirrels, &c. These animals are distinguished by their having no canine teeth, and by having their incisors or cutting teeth large, curved and sharp. The lower jaw has two of these sharp teeth; the upper jaw in some cases two and in others four. A peculiarity of these front teeth is that they are not covered with enamel on the inner side, so that constant use wears away the bone and maintains a sharp cutting edge. Hence they are called gnawing animals. Of those having two incisor teeth in the upper jaw, many specimens are exhibited among which are :—

SQUIRRELS—

The Common Squirrel—(*Sciurus vulgaris*).

The Sharp-nosed Squirrel—(*S. laticaudatus*) from Borneo.

The Bajing—(*S. plantani*) from Java.

The Carolina Squirrel—(*S. carolinensis*) from North America.

The Blackbanded Tupai—(*S. nigrovittatus*) from Java.

The Brazilian Squirrel—(*S. æstivans*) from Brazil.

The Chickaree—(*S. hudsonius*) from North America.

The Grey Squirrel—(*S. cinereus*) from North America.

The Italian Squirrel—(*S. italicus*) from Tuscany.

The Western Grey Squirrel—(*S. fossor*) from California.

The Tamias—(*Tamias striatus*) from North America.

Townsend's Striped Squirrel—(*Tamias townsendi*) from California.

The Flying Squirrel—(*Sciuropterus volucella*) from Canada.

The Marmot—(*Arctomys marmotta*) from Switzerland.

BEAVERS—(*Castor*) Northern Europe and America.

DORMICE—

The Dormouse—(*Myoxus avellanarius*) from Europe.

RATS and MICE—

The Common Rat—(*Mus decumanus*).

The Common Mouse—(*Mus musculus*).

The Field Mouse—(*Mus sylvaticus*) from Canada.

The Alpine Arvicole—(*Arvicola nivalis*) from Switzerland.

The Water Rat—(*Arvicola amphibius*) from Britain.

The Musquash—(*Fiber zibethicus*) from North America.

The Jerboa—(*Dipus œgyptius*) from Egypt, (*D. jagulus*) from Africa, and (*D. gerboa*).

The Hamster—(*Cricetus*) from N. America, and (*C. frumentarius*) from Europe.

PORCUPINES—

The Porcupine—(*Hystrix cristata*) from Africa and Asia.

The Tree Porcupine—(*Synetheres insidiosus*) from Granada, South America.

GUINEA PIGS—

The Guinea Pig—(*Cavia aperea*) from Brazil.

The Golden Agouti—(*Dasyprocta aguti*) from South America.

The Coypu or Racoonda—(*Myopotamus coypus*) from Central America.

Of those that have four incisor teeth in the upper jaw there are shown—

RABBITS—

The Rabbit—(*Lepus cuniculus*) from Europe.

The Hare—(*Lepus timidus*) from Europe.

The Black-necked Rabbit—(*L. nigricollis*) from North America.

The Snow or Mountain Hare—(*L. variabilis*) from Scandanavia. Rabbits and Hares are common all over Europe, and a white variety of the latter is found in Scandanavia, Scotland and Ireland.

Order VII.—UNGULATA, or HOOFED ANIMALS.

—This order includes such diverse forms as the Elephant, Rhinoceros, Horse, Pig, Camel, Ox, Deer, Sheep, etc. They are mostly of large size and well known. The common feature which groups them together is the hoof, a horny covering enclosing and protecting the last joint of the toes. The front teeth are sometimes wanting, but the molars are broad and flat, suitable for grinding, as all the Ungulata are vegetable feeders, except Pigs, which are omnivorous. With such a variety of animals in one order it is necessary to classify them into Sub-orders, and for this purpose several methods have been proposed.

The following is that in use at the British Museum :—

Sub-Order I.—Proboscidea : Elephants.

    II.—Hydracoidea : Coneys.

    III.—Perissodactyla : Rhinoceroses, Tapirs, Horses, Asses

    IV.—Artiodactyla ;

        Section 1. *Suina :* Pigs, Hippopotamus.

          2. *Tylopoda :* Camels and Llamas.

          3. *Tragulina :* Chevrotains.

          4. *Pecora :* Oxen, Antelopes, Deer, Sheep, etc.

The specimens of Ungulata in this Museum are not arranged in accordance with this or any other plan as space does not permit it, but they are mostly large and can easily be found.

Sub-Order I.—Proboscidea, consists only of the Elephants, of which there are two living species — the Indian Elephant, and the African Elephant. They have no canine teeth, but their incisor teeth grow to a great length and form the tusks, and their molar teeth are few but large. The trunk, or proboscis, is however the peculiar feature of the Elephant ; it is both nose and hand to its possessor and is an organ of great delicacy of touch. Elephants have broad flat feet with five toes encased in a common hoof. A skeleton is exhibited in the Osteological Hall. The extinct Mammoth and Mastodon belonged to this order.

Sub-Order II.—Hydracoidea, contains only the Coneys, small animals found in Africa and Arabia. These are sometimes classed with the Rhinoceros in the next order. The only specimen in the Museum is a *Hyrax*, of which a skeleton is exhibited in the Osteological Hall.

Sub-Order III.—Perissodactyla. The name of this order is derived from the Greek *perissos* odd and *daktylos* a finger, and implies that the animals composing it have an odd number of toes, one or three, on each hind foot. The existing genera are widely separated in other respects, but fossil forms complete the series and justify their being grouped together.

The **Rhinoceroses** (*Rhinoceros sondaicus* and *Ceratorhinus sumatrensis*), on the floor of the Central Hall, are natives of Java and Sumatra, where they live in the marshes and swamps. They have three toes on each foot; species of the former genus have one horn, the latter two, placed on the snout. There are mounted specimens on the floor of the Central Hall, and also a skeleton in the Osteological Hall.

The **Tapir** (*Tapirus sumatranus*) is in a case; and (*T. leucogenys*), is on floor of Central Hall. These are usually nocturnal in their habits and are found in the swamps and rivers of South-eastern Asia, and of South America. Their snout is prolonged till it may be called a short trunk.

The **Horse**. The genus *Equus* includes wild and domesticated horses of all kinds, asses, and zebras. These have one toe only in use on each foot, corresponding to our middle finger, and they walk on the point of it. A skeleton of a horse is exhibited on the first landing of the staircase.

The **Zebra** (*Equus burchelli*) to be seen on the floor of the Central Hall, is a native of South Africa. Two mounted specimens are exhibited, and a skeleton is in the end case of the Osteological Hall.

Sub-Order IV.—Artiodactyla (derived from Gr. *artios*, even; *daktylos*, a finger), implies that the number of toes on each foot is even—two or four. This sub-order is again divided into non-ruminant and ruminant animals. In the former the teeth have tuberculated crowns; in the latter they are crescent shaped.

THE NON-RUMINANTS are the Pigs or Boars and the Hippopotamus.

Section I., Suina. The Pigs have four toes visible, two of which are covered by hoofs, but the other two are not fully developed; they have a long snout capable of considerable motion, and very small eyes. In some of the Wild Pigs the canine teeth grow into large curved tusks. In America the Pigs are represented by the Peccaries, which differ in a few respects from the true Pigs, and are much smaller. Specimens exhibited are :—

The Wild Boar—(*Sus scrofa*) of Europe.

The Wild Pig—(*Sus papuensis*) of New Guinea.

The Collared Peccary—(*Dicotyles tajaçu*) from S. America.

The Hippopotamus—(*H. amphibius*) a native of Africa, where it is called the River Horse. Its teeth are very powerful, especially the canines, which have sharp chisel like edges. A skeleton may be seen in the Osteological Hall.

THE RUMINANTS are the most important of all to man, as the majority of our domestic and food-supplying animals belong to this group. They are distinguished by their complicated stomachs. They have, as a rule, no front teeth in the upper jaw. The stomach of a ruminant consists of four parts, sometimes called separate stomachs. The first receives the food direct from the mouth, moistens it with certain fluids, and passes it on to the second stomach ; this is a small bag which rolls the food in balls and returns it to the mouth ; it is then leisurely chewed and mixed with the saliva—a process known as " chewing the cud "—and once more swallowed, this time passing into the third stomach ; here the proper digestive processes are continued, and finally the food is passed on to the fourth stomach, whence it goes into the intestines. The ruminants include Camels, Oxen, Sheep, Goats, Deer, etc.

Section II.—Tylopoda. The Camels are found in Central Asia and North-eastern Africa. They have long necks, very broad and flat feet, humps* on the back, and a more than usually complicated stomach. They are invaluable as beasts of burden in sandy countries within or near the tropics, and have been introduced into Australia for that purpose, but they are often ill-tempered and not easily managed. Allied to the Camels are the Llamas of South America. There is a skeleton of a Bactrian Camel (*Camelus bactrianus*), from the Himalayas, in the Entrance Hall, and a mounted Llama (*Lama peruana*), temporarily in a case in the "Old Wing."

---

* The True Camel or Dromedary has one hump, the Bactrian Camel two.

Section III.—Tragulina. The Chevrotains are pretty little animals like miniature goats, but no larger than a terrier dog, and are found in Southern India. In a case in the "Old Wing" are specimens of the Musk Deer or Napu (*Tragulus javanicus*) from Java.

Section IV.—Pecora, contains the *Bovidæ*, *Cervidæ*, and *Camelopardalidæ*.

The BOVIDÆ include Goats, Oxen, Buffaloes, Sheep, Antelopes, &c.; all of which are too well known to need description here. The following specimens are exhibited :—

The Gaur or Wild Ox—(*Bos gaurus*) from India, in Central Hall.

The Sheep—(*Ovis aries*).

The Goat—(*Capra hirca*).

The Sœmmerring's Antelope—(*Gazella sœmmerringi*) from Abyssinia.

The Pronghorn—(*Antilocapra americana*) from the prairie lands of N. America.

The Indian Antelope—(*Cervicapra bezoartica*) from India.

The Gnu—(*Catoblepas taurina*) from South Africa, in Central Hall.

The Sable Antelope—(*Hippotragus niger*) from South Africa, in Australian Hall.

The Oryx—(*Oryx leucoryx*) from Africa.

The Chamois—(*Rupicapra tragus*) from Switzerland.

The Sassaybi Antelope — (*Ægocerus lunatus*) from South Africa, in Central Hall.

The Blaue Bok—(*Ægocerus leucophæus*) from Africa, in Central Hall.

The Grys Bok—(*Neotragus melanotis*) from Africa.

The Spring Bok—(*Antidorcas euchore*) from Africa.

The CAMELOPARDALIDÆ contain but a single species.

The Giraffe—(*Camelopardalis giraffa*) from Africa, skeleton in Central Hall.

The CERVIDÆ consist of the antlered ruminants only, such as the Deer. In the Bovidæ the horns grow over a projection on the bone of the skull, are never shed, and are not branched. In the Cervidæ, horns, strictly speaking, are not present, but are replaced by antlers, which grow from the skull, are covered with a delicate skin while growing, and are shed annually; the males only possess antlers, except in the case of the Reindeer. The following species are represented :—

The Muntjak—(*Cervulus sclateri* and *Cervulus muntjak*) from India.

The Red Deer or Stag—(*Cervus elephas*) from Germany and Ireland.

The Roe Deer—(*Capreolus caprœa*) from Scotland, found also in Europe.

The Spotted Deer—(*Axis maculata*) from India.

The Irish "Elk"—now extinct—(*Megaceros hibernicus*) a skeleton of which from Ireland, is in the Osteological Hall.

Orders VIII and IX.—CETACEA and SIRENIA.—

These two orders were formerly considered as one, but a knowledge of their structural differences have now led zoologists to separate them. The *Cetacea* comprise most of the aquatic Mammals :—Whales, Porpoises, and Dolphins. The *Sirenia* contain the Manatees, and Dugongs, and the now extinct *Rhytina stelleri.*

The largest living animal known is the Whale, of which there are many species. On account of its large size only skeletons can be preserved and shown in a museum. The principal are :—

The Baleen Whales, of which the Greenland Whale (*Balœna mysticetus*) is perhaps the best known. Its characteristic is the "whalebone" which serves as a strainer to separate the food from the water when it fills its mouth. The Greenland Whale is a native of the Arctic Ocean. It sometimes attains a length of 80 feet, and is hunted for its Whalebone and Oil. It is not found in Southern Seas, and there is no specimen in this Museum, but smaller species of *Balœna* or Whalebone Whales exist here. Some of these, of which skeletons are exhibited, are :—

Balæna antipodarum.

Balæna novæ-zealandiæ.

Balænoptera marginalis.

The Sperm Whale (*Physeter macrocephalus*) is of equal importance in commerce to the Baleen Whale on account of the spermaceti found in the cavity of the head, and the sperm oil from its blubber. Its mouth is not provided with whalebone, but has permanent teeth in the lower jaw. There is a skeleton supported overhead in the Australian Hall. The whale, from which it was taken, was caught off Wollongong in November 1860, and was over 70 feet long. Over the cases in the same Hall are specimens of smaller species of Sperm Whales—

Mesoplodon thomsonii,
Dioplodon seychellensis, } both very rare species.

and in the Osteological Hall other skeletons and skulls will be found, including several of the rarer species, as Gray's Whale (*Kogia breviceps*), &c.

The Dolphins and Porpoises also belong to the order Cetacea. The common Dolphin (*Delphinus*) is found in the Atlantic and Mediterranean, but a species closely resembling it occurs on the Australian coast and elsewhere, while other species or varieties are found all over the world. The Porpoise differs slightly from the Dolphin in outward appearance but chiefly in the shape of its head and form of its teeth. The species which is familiar to boatmen in Port Jackson is however a Dolphin, having teeth in both jaws. The "Killer" (*Orca*) is the Grampus. Mounted specimens are to be seen in the Central Hall, Upper floor. Skeletons of Dolphins, Porpoises, and Grampuses are also to be found in the Osteological Hall.

The Manatees and Dugongs form the order Sirenia (from the Greek *Seiren* a Mermaid), and are very peculiar animals. They inhabit the estuaries of the large rivers and the bays of the tropics. There are skeletons of two species of Manatees and one of the Dugong in the Osteological Hall, and mounted specimens in the Central Hall, Upper floor.

The Manatee—(*Manatus australis*) of South America, and (*M. senegalensis*) of Western Africa.

The Dugong (*Halicore dugong*) is found as far south as Moreton Bay on the Queensland coast, and westwards through the Indian Ocean to the east coast of Africa, inhabiting shallow waters of bays and inlets and feeding on sea-weed. When adult it may be as much as 10 feet in length; the colour of the smooth glossy back varies from flesh colour to light brown, the under surface being lighter. The full-grown males have a pair of conspicuous tusks in the upper jaws, which are not developed in the females. The flesh is valued as food by the natives; the oil is of excellent quality, and has been used with good results as a substitute for cod-liver oil; but the number of the animals is limited, and the fishery is yearly becoming less productive.

The Rhytina—(*Rhytina stelleri*) of Alaska. This species is now extinct, but a skeleton (not quite perfect), and some casts have been obtained for this Museum. It was the largest of the Sirenia, sometimes measuring 25 feet long. It was formerly abundant at Behring's Strait. The head was small in proportion to the body. The neck was short, the body rapidly diminishing behind. The short fore arm terminated abruptly without fingers or nails, and was overgrown with a short stiff brush of hair, the hind legs being replaced by a whale-like fluke. The animal was destitute of teeth, but instead was provided with two masticating oral plates, one in the upper, the other in the lower jaw.[*]

Order X.—EDENTATA.—The word Edentata is used by naturalists to signify toothless mammals. This order includes the Sloths, Ant-eaters, etc., which are peculiar to South America and Africa. The Sloths are animals with long curved claws suited for tree-climbing, but not at all suited for walking on the ground. Existing species seldom exceed three feet in length, but in ancient times gigantic species existed, as witness the *Megatherium* (see Chapter XIV. Palæontology). The Anteaters have long pointed snouts, and a narrow tongue which they shoot out rapidly to a considerable distance to capture the ants, on which, as their name implies, they feed. The Armadilloes are the most remarkable of the Edentata. Their bodies are covered with horn-like plates or scales, on the back and over the tail and joints, while the bellies are only protected by ordinary soft hairy skin. A few species of Edentata are found in other parts of the world —the Pangolins of Asia, and the Aard-varks of Africa—but they differ in many respects from the South American species.

---

[*] Voyage of the *Vega*. Vol. 2, p. 272.

The following specimens are exhibited in the Museum—

The Sloth—(*Bradypus torquatus*) from South America.

The Armadillo—(*Tatusia peba*)from Central and South America.

The Hairy or True Anteater—(*Myrmecophaga tetradactyla,* and *M. didactyla*) from South America.

The Scaly Anteater or Pangolin—(*Manis pentadactyla*) from India, (*M. tetradactyla* and *M. longicaudata*) from Africa.

The Great Manis—(*Pholidotus giganteus*) from Africa.

The Aard Vark or Cape Ant Bear—(*Orycteropus capensis*) from Africa.

Orders XI and XII.—MARSUPIALIA and MONO-TREMATA.

—These orders include the Kangaroos, and most of the other Australian mammals, and as they are for the most part peculiar to the Australian region they are of special interest to visitors to this Museum. A chapter will therefore be devoted to these alone (Chapter V.). The peculiarity which groups these animals together is the presence of certain bones, known as the "marsupial bones," which are always accompanied by a more or less well defined pouch, in which the female carries her young after birth until they are able to take care of themselves.

We say the Marsupials are peculiar to Australia, but there is one exception—the Opossum—which is found in America. This is a pretty little animal with a long nose, naked tail, and feet fitted for tree-climbing. The Virginian Opossum was the first discovered marsupial, known long before the Australian species were found. A specimen (*Didelphis cancrivora*) is to be seen in the Museum.

V.

AUSTRALIAN MAMMALIA.

ORDER MARSUPIALIA.—Australia is remarkable for an order of animals almost peculiarly its own—the Marsupials—which have no living representatives elsewhere, if we except the single family which contains the true Opossums (*Didelphidæ*), found in America (see page 38). The name is derived from the Latin *marsupium*, a pouch, and is given to these animals because the females of all species are provided with a pouch, into which they convey the young immediately after birth, and in which they nurse them until they are capable of caring for themselves. Marsupials are brought forth at a much earlier stage of development than is usual among mammals, and when first placed in the pouch they adhere so firmly to the nipples as to give some apparent foundation for the popular error that they grow there like buds on a tree. The skeleton has the general characteristics of all mammals, but is peculiar in having also what are known as the "marsupial bones," which consist of a pair of small bones attached to the pelvis, supposed to support the pouch. The skull is elongate, and the brain large ; the angle of the lower jaw is bent inwards ; and there are other peculiarities which will be noticed under the different species.

The Marsupials include Herbivorous, Carnivorous, and Insectivorous forms. In other words the land Mammals of Australia, with the exception of the Dingo, the indigenous Rats and Mice, and the Bats, are all Marsupials, and have become adapted to widely different habits and modes of life, some being herbivorous, some frugivorous, some insectivorous, some carnivorous, some fleet runners, and some living habitually in trees. There are, however, if we except the Tasmanian Tiger, no large carnivorous mammals among them. Some remarkable fossil forms have been discovered, which are described in chapter XIV. Palæontology ; our Australian animals are in fact living representatives of races which in former eras peopled the whole world.

There are seven families of Marsupials, six of which are found in Australia and New Guinea, and the remaining one on the American Continent.

The following table shows the Families and Genera into which the existing forms of the Order MARSUPIALIA are divided :—

Family I. Macropodidæ—Macropus ; Osphranter ; Halmaturus ; Petrogale ; Dendrolagus ; Dorcopsis ; Onychogale ; Lagorchestes ; Bettongia ; Hypsiprymnus.

Family II. Pleiopodidæ—Hypsiprymnodon.

Family III. Peramelidæ—Perameles ; Peragale ; Chœropus.

Family IV. Phalangistidæ — Phalangista ; Cuscus ; Petaurista ; Belideus ; Acrobata ; Dromicia ; Tarsipes.

Family V. Dasyuridæ—Thylacinus ; Sarcophilus ; Dasyurus. ; Phascologale ; Antechinus ; Podabrus ; Antechinomys.

Family VI. Phascolomyidæ—Phascolomys ; Phascolarctos.

Family VII. Didelphidæ—Didelphys ; Chironectes (American).

FAMILY 1.—MACROPODIDÆ or Kangaroos. The members of this family are distinguished by their long hind legs, very short fore legs, and powerful tails ; their usual mode of progression is by leaps in which only the hind legs touch the ground, and the tail oscillates up and down as a balance or counterpoise to the body ; they attain a considerable speed, and it requires a good horse to surpass them ; a large kangaroo has been known to leap 25 feet in one bound.

In the hind foot of the Kangaroos the first toe is wanting ; the second and third are very slender and enclosed in a common skin, appearing outwardly like one toe with a double nail ; the fourth is very large and encased in a strong pointed claw—it is the principal part of the foot; the fifth toe also is in a sheath but is much smaller. The foot has thus the appearance of having one large and two small toes. The fore feet have each the usual five toes of nearly uniform size.

Kangaroos are also distinguished by the end of the nose being hairy, and the eyes having eyelashes, as they are the only marsupials that move about and feed in the daytime; the head being long and narrow; and the pouch opening forward. The usual number of teeth is 20 in the upper jaw and 14 in the lower arranged thus :— incisors $\frac{0}{9}$; canines $\frac{0}{0}$, or $\frac{1\cdot1}{1\cdot1}$; premolars $\frac{2\cdot2}{1\cdot1}$; molars $\frac{4\cdot4}{4\cdot4}$; Total $\frac{18}{12}$ or $\frac{20}{14}$.*

The front or incisor teeth are powerful, but the others are small. They are vegetable feeders, eating grass and leaves. In size they vary from the great black Kangaroo, 6 feet high, to the Rat Kangaroo, which can go into one's pocket.

The Kangaroo was discovered by Captain Cook in 1770, and first described in Dr. Hawkesbury's account of the Voyage. The earliest name given to it was *Yerboa gigantea*, which was considered inappropriate, and the name *Macropus*, given by Dr. Shaw in 1790, is now used. *Macropus* is from the Greek, *makros*, large and *pous*, a foot. *Kangaroo* was supposed to be the native name.

The specimens of Kangaroos in the Museum are exhibited in the "Australian Hall" in cases Nos. 1, 2, 3 and 4. The following are some of the principal species.

Macropus major; the great Grey Kangaroo found all over N.S,W., South and West Australia, and Tasmania. In a full grown specimen the skull is 7 or 8 inches long, and the animal itself often 6 feet high.

M. ocydromus; a form closely resembling *M. major* found in West Australia.

M. erubescens; a rare species from South Australia.

M. parryi; a pretty silver-grey kangaroo found in the central parts of N.S.W., and known as Parry's Kangaroo.

---

* For explanation of formula see in Chapter XIII. Osteology.

Osphranter antilopinus; this animal has shorter hind legs than *Macropus*, but a larger central toe; the hair is hard, and the head and muzzle broader. (There is not a specimen of *O. antilopinus* in the Museum at present.)

O. rufus; the male of this has short, woolly fur of a bright rusty colour. The female is light grey.

O. robustus; the Black Wallaroo or great Rock Kangaroo of N.S.W., is a slate colour in the male, and grey in the female.

Halmaturus dorsalis; the Black Striped Wallaby of N.S.W. and Queensland.

H. agilis; inhabits the scrub in the Northern Territory. The fur is coarse and the colour a yellowish brown.

H. ruficollis; so called on account of its red neck; is a native of N.S.W., and is the most common of the genus. It was first discovered by Péron and Lesueur on King Island.

H. bennettii; Bennett's Wallaby; the Brush Kangaroo of Tasmania. It is supposed to be a variety of *H. ruficollis* although somewhat darker in colour.

H. thetidis; the Pademelon of N.S.W. This is a pretty Wallaby, with long soft fur. One was taken to Paris alive by the "Thetis."

H. manicatus (or irma); the Black Gloved Wallaby of West Australia.

H. ualabatus; the Black Wallaby of N.S.W. The animal itself is brown—only the feet and tail are black.

H. parma; is a reddish-coloured Wallaby found in N.S.W.

H. derbianus; Derby's Wallaby, West Australia.

H. brachyurus; the Short Tailed Wallaby of West Australia.

H. crassipes; a New Guinea Wallaby from Port Moresby.

H. mastersi ; Masters' Wallaby, Queensland.

H. greyi ; from South Australia, named after Captain George Grey.

H. wilcoxi ; from the Richmond and Clarence Rivers district.

H. brownii ; a Wallaby from New Ireland.

H. billardieri ; the Tasmanian Wallaby.

Petrogale penicillata ; the Rock Wallaby of N. S. W.

P xanthopus ; a yellow-footed Rock Wallaby from Flinder's Range, South Australia.

P. longicaudata ; Long-tailed Rock Wallaby, N. S. W.

P. sp. ; from Derby, West Australia.

Dendrolagus ursinus ; D. inustus and D. dorianus ; these are Kangaroos with the anterior extremities large and powerful and with large foreclaws ; they are found in New Guinea, and two other species are found in Queensland.

Dorcopsis luctuosa ; is a Wallaby found in New Guinea. It differs from other genera in its dentition.

Onychogale unguifer ; is a Kangaroo from the North West and other parts of Australia, it is of a slender and graceful form, about the size of a rabbit, of a pale red colour, and is characterised by the horny point to its tail, from which it is called the nail-tailed kangaroo.

O. lunata ; is from West Australia.

O. frenata ; is from the lower Murray district, N. S. W.

Lagorchestes leporoides ; the Hare Kangaroo, found in South and West Australia and in N. S. W. This is a very active little animal, with small and delicate feet and velvety fur. It differs from the Great Kangaroo in its upper teeth. The name is derived from the Greek *lagos* a hare and *orchestes*, a dancer.

L. fasciatus ; from West Australia.

L. leichardti ; from West Australia.

L. conspicillatus ; from N. W. Australia.

L. hirsutus ; from West Australia.

Bettongia rufescens ; the Rat Kangaroo, so called from its small size. This species is found in N. S. W.

B. ogilbii ; from West Australia.

B. penicillata ; from N. S. W.

B. cuniculus ; from Tasmania.

B. grayi ; from West Australia, and N. S. W.

B. campestris ; from South Australia.

Hypsiprymnus murinus ; a pretty little animal with long dark fur found in N. S. W.

H. apicalis ; also found in N. S. W.

H. platyops ⎱
H. gilberti ⎰ both from West Australia.

FAMILY 2.—PLEIOPODIDÆ — There is only one genus known as yet in this family ; it is a little animal, in all respects like the smaller kangaroos except in the toes, of which it has five fully developed. It has been described and named by Dr. Ramsay,

Hypsiprymnodon moschatus ; from specimens found at Rockingham Bay, Queensland. It is regarded by Prof. Owen as forming the type, not merely of a new genus, but of a new family.

FAMILY 3.—PERAMELIDÆ or Bandicoots.—The animals comprising this family in outward appearance resemble rabbits or small kangaroos, but in the fore feet some of the toes are rudimentary while the hind feet are like the kangaroo's. They have six incisor teeth in the lower jaw, whereas the kangaroos have only two. The tail is short. The pouch opens backwards, that is, towards the tail. The usual arrangement of the teeth is:—incisors $\frac{5 \cdot 0}{\cdot}$; canines $\frac{1 \cdot 1}{1 \cdot 1}$; premolars $\frac{3 \cdot 3}{3 \cdot 3}$; molars $\frac{4 \cdot 4}{4 \cdot 4}$ total $\frac{2 \; 6}{2 \; 2}$. They are vegetable-feeders. The Bandicoots represented in the Museum are in cases 5 and 6. The principal species are :—

Perameles gunni; Gunn's Bandicoot, from Tasmania. This was the first species described.

P. broadbenti; Broadbent's Bandicoot, from New Guinea.

P. nasuta; the long-nosed Bandicoot of N.S.W.

P. myosurus; the saddle-backed Bandicoot of Western Australia.

P. fasciata; the striped Bandicoot from South Australia.

P. moresbiensis; Port Moresby Bandicoot.

P. cockerelli; a Bandicoot from New Ireland.

Peragale lagotis; sometimes called the Rabbit-rat. This animal is rather different from the Perameles; it has very long ears and long soft fur. It is found in N.S.W. and in South Australia.

Chœropus castanotis; a peculiar little animal like a rat with the feet of a pig, that is, with two toes only on the fore feet, while the hind foot has one well-developed toe. It has a soft grey or brown fur.

FAMILY 4.—PHALANGISTIDÆ—These are also vegetable feeders, living on grass, leaves and young shoots. They are good climbers and most of them have long prehensile tails, with which they can swing themselves from branch to branch; in some species, however, the tail is wanting. There are five toes on each foot, the second and third toes on the hind feet are united with a common skin. The arrangement of the teeth is:—incisors $\frac{6}{2}$; canines $\frac{1 \cdot 1}{1 \cdot 1}$ or $\frac{1 \cdot 1}{0 \cdot 0}$; premolars $\frac{1 \cdot 1}{1 \cdot 1}$; molars $\frac{4 \cdot 4}{4 \cdot 4}$ or $\frac{3 \cdot 3}{3 \cdot 3}$; which allows for considerable variation. They are all nocturnal in their habits. Specimens are in cases 5 and 6.

Group 1.—Phalangistinæ; Phalangers, or Austialian Opossums, are found all over Australia. They have long prehensile tails. The Phalangistas proper are natives of Australia and Tasmania; the Cuscus are natives of the islands north of Australia. The tail of the Cuscus is often devoid of hair. They are not really Opossums, but are so called from their resemblance to the true Opossum, which is a native of America. The principal specimens are :—

Phalangista cookii (or Cook's Phalanger) was discovered by Sir Joseph Banks on Capt. Cook's first voyage to Australia.

P. laniginosa, the Woolly Phalanger (or Ring Tailed Opossum), a native of N.S.W.

P. fuliginosa; the Sooty Phalanger, of Tasmania; is distinguished by its long bushy tail and black fur.

P. vulpina; the Vulpine Opossum found in Tasmania and N.S.W.

P. viverrina; Viverrine Phalanger, from Western Australia.

P. canina; the Canine Opossum of New South Wales; has grey fur and a black tail.

Cuscus chrysorrhous; the New Guinea Opossum.

C. orientalis; from New Ireland and the Solomon Islands. The native name of this species in the island of Amboyna is said to be Coes-Coes.

C. maculatus; the Spotted Phalanger, from Cape York.

C. brevicaudatus; also from Cape York.

Dactylopsila trivirgata; from Rockingham Bay, Cape York, and New Guinea.

Dromicia gliriformis, is a very small species, with soft grey fur and large eyes. It feeds on honey from the Eucalyptus flowers and Banksias, and partly hybernates in winter.

Group 2.—Petauristinæ; Flying Phalangers. The tail in this group is very long, but not prehensile. There is a membrane between the fore and hind legs which adapts the animal for flight.

Petaurista taguanoides ; the Great Flying Phalanger, a native of N.S.W. Its fur is long and soft, brown above and dull white beneath.

Belideus ariel, from Cape York and New Guinea.

B. breviceps ; the Short Headed Flying Phalanger of N.S.W.

B. flaviventer ; from N.S.W.

B. sciurus ; the Squirrel-like Flying Phalanger, from Queensland, and N.S.W.

Acrobata pygmæa ; the Opossum Mouse from N.S.W., and the smallest of the tribe.

Group 3.—Phascolarctinæ ; the Koala or Native Bear. These are quiet, peaceable animals ; their fur is very thick and soft, generally grey in colour. Their favourite food is the leaves of the Eucalypti, though they eat some kinds of roots and in confinement will live a short time on bread and vegetables. The young is carried on the mother's back till it is able to climb alone. There are several examples in cases 9 and 10.

Phascolarctos cinereus, is the only known species.

Group 4.—Tarsipedinæ.

Tarsipes rostratus ; this animal is remarkably different from others in the family. It is about the size of a mouse, has very small teeth, a sharp nose and long tail, it has also five toes on each foot ; it is a native of Western Australia, and lives on honey obtained from the proteaceous plants.

FAMILY 5.—DASYURIDÆ.—The members of this family are carnivorous ; they live on birds and eggs, insects, and other mammals. The feet are of the usual marsupial type, viz. : five toes in the front and four in the hind feet, the second and third toes of the hind feet are, however, not united, and the tail is not prehensile. They have eight incisors in the upper and six in the lower jaws, and seven molars in each jaw. The specimens are to be seen in cases 7, 8, and 9.

Dasyurus viverrinus; the Native Cat of N.S.W., and Tasmania.

D. maculatus ; the Tiger Cat of Tasmania, Victoria & N.S.W.

D. geoffroyi ; Geoffroy's Dasyure from South and West Australia.

D. hallucatus ; the slender tailed Dasyure of North Australia is the smallest of the genus.

D. gracilis ; from Queensland.

Sarcophilus ursinus ; the Tasmanian Devil. This is now confined to Tasmania.

Thylacinus cynocephalus ; the Tasmanian Tiger or Wolf is the largest of the *Dasyuridæ.* In outward appearance this very much resembles a dog ; it was in past ages an inhabitant of Australia, where its fossil remains are still found. It is now found alive only in Tasmania, and even there it is fast being exterminated.

Phascologale penicillata ; the Ring-tailed Rat of Western Australia and of N. S. W. is a little animal smaller than the *D. hallucatus* mentioned above. It chiefly lives on eggs, young birds, and insects. There are other species of *Phascologale* not represented in the collection.

Chætocercrus cristicaudatus ; from South Australia, (type specimen).

Antechinus ; There are several species of these pretty little animals in the cases. Representatives of the genus are found all over Australia. In size and appearance they are very like the common mouse, but in structure and habits very different.

Antechinus Swainsoni ; Tasmania.

A. unicolor ; N.S.W.

A. flavipes ; N.S.W.

A. apicalis ; South and West Australia.

A. albipes ; West Australia.

A. fuliginosus ; West Australia.

A. murinus ; N.S.W.

A. maculatus ; Queensland.

Podabrus macrurus ; from Queensland.

Antechinomys lanigera ; from N.S.W

Myrmecobius fasciatus ; the Australian Ant-eater. This is a gentle, easily tamed animal, with a long, slender tongue formed for licking up ants, a pointed snout, short, strong legs, and a bushy tail. It is peculiar in having an unusually large number of teeth, their arrangement being $\frac{4 \cdot 4}{3 \cdot 3}$; $\frac{1 \cdot 1}{1 \cdot 1}$; $\frac{8 \cdot 8}{9 \cdot 9}$; Total, 52. The female has no pouch.

FAMILY 6. — PHASCOLOMYIDÆ, or Wombats, are different in many respects from other marsupials. They have stout bodies, large heads, and small eyes. Each foot has five toes, furnished (except the first toe of the hind foot) with broad, solid nails or claws, to burrow for the roots on which they feed. Their tail is so short as to be entirely hidden by the fur. The teeth are : Incisors, $\frac{2}{2}$; premolars, $\frac{1 \cdot 1}{1 \cdot 1}$; molars, $\frac{4 \cdot 4}{4 \cdot 4}$; Total, $1\frac{3}{2}$, all without roots, and only fixed in the gums. The specimens are in cases 1 and 2 under the Kangaroos. There are also bones of fossil species in the Osteological collection.

Phascolomys wombat is the common species. It is found in New South Wales, Western Australia, and Tasmania. It is a nocturnal animal, growing to over 3 feet in length and 60 lbs. in weight.

P. latifrons, from South Australia, has marked differences in the teeth.

FAMILY 7.— DIDELPHIDÆ, or true Opossums, are natives of America. (See page 38.)

Order MONOTREMATA.—This order also is peculiar to Australia and the Austro-Malayan sub-region, and may be called one of the wonders of the world. It forms a connecting link between the mammals, the birds, and the reptiles, having features common to each. The Monotremes lay eggs like birds or reptiles, hatch them, and suckle their young like mammals, and nurse them like marsupials. They were originally classed with the marsupials ; but the differences are so great that they are now placed in a separate order by themselves. The marsupial bones are present but the pouch is said to be wanting in the Platypus, and found in the Echidna only when she has eggs or young, and there are considerable differences in the brain and in the skeleton. There are two genera of Echidnidæ, but only one of

Platypus; specimens are to be seen in case 10.   Bones of a very large fossil species of Echidna have been found in the Wellington caves.

Ornithorhynchus paradoxus; the Platypus.   This has a bill like a duck and webbed feet for swimming, the fore feet also have claws for burrowing.   It has short velvety fur; it lives in the water and makes its nest in holes in the bank; it feeds on larvæ, and minute aquatic animals which it finds in the water and in the mud; it has 8 horny teeth; it grows to about 18 inches in length.

Tachyglossus aculeatus; the Australian Porcupine, or Echidna.   This is about the size of the Platypus, which also it resembles in most of its internal structure, but is covered with spines like a porcupine on the back, with coarse hair intermixed.   It is not a water animal, but lives on land and feeds on insects.   It has a long snout, with a small opening for the mouth, and a round slender sticky tongue with which it secures its food.   The feet have very strong claws, by which the animal can bury itself in the ground very quickly.   It has been known to penetrate two feet of loose garden soil in two or three minutes.   There is a spine on the hind legs of the male connected with a gland.   From this the name *Echidna* (Greek, a viper) is derived, as it was erroneously supposed to be poisonous.   Other species are :—

T. setosa ; Tasmania.   This species has shorter spines and more hair than the others.

T. lawesii ; New Guinea.

Acanthoglossus bruyni; New Guinea.   Casts of the skull and lower jaw of this species are to be seen in the Museum

Other orders—PLACENTALS.—Although Australia is the home of the Marsupials and Monotremes, other orders are not altogether unrepresented.   There are no Monkeys, and few large Carnivora; the hoofed animals, as the Horse, Rhinoceros, Deer, &c., are wanting, as are also the Edentata, or toothless animals. The following are, however, represented :—

CANIDÆ or DOGS.

Canis dingo ; the Native Dog. It is a moot point whether or not the Dingo is indigenous or has been introduced by man. There is evidence of its having been in the country before the arrival of the first white settlers, so that it must have come from the very early navigators or by way of the Northern Islands and Torres Straits. The real Native Dog, however, is called by the aborigines the Worregal, and the Dingo is only the black man's name for the white man's dog. There are specimens in case 11.

PINNIPEDIA or SEALS.

Arctocephalus cinereus, the Eared Seal commonly found on the coast of N.S.W.

Stenorhynchus leptonyx, the Sea Leopard

Specimens are to be seen in case 11, and in the Central Hall, Upper Floor (see pages 26 and 27).

INSECTIVOROUS BATS.—The insect-eating Bats found in Australia are represented in the Museum by the following genera:

Molossus; Plecotus; Taphozous; Nyctophilus; Vespertilio; Vesperugo; Patalia; Rhinolophus; and **Scotophilus.**

FRUIT-EATING BATS are represented by :—

Pteropus, the flying fox; and **Harpyia** and others, from New Guinea (see page 28).

RODENTIA. Of this Order the Rats only are indigenous to Australia. These are well represented by various species, in case No. 11, of MUS, or ground Rats; HYDROMYS, or Water Rats, said to be peculiar to Australia and New Guinea; and HAPALOTIS, or Tree Rats, which construct nests in trees or among dense vines.

CETACEA ; Whales (see page 35).

SIRENIA ; Dugongs (see page 36).

VI.

BIRDS.

BIRDS, like mammals, are air-breathing animals, with a back-bone and four limbs,—feet and wings, though in some cases the latter are not used for flying. In species adapted for flight the bones are hollow or cellular, combining strength with lightness. In living birds the temperature of the blood is much higher than in mammals, reaching sometimes 110°. Some fossil forms of birds resemble reptiles in certain respects, and Prof. Huxley has therefore grouped them together in a division called *Sauropsida.*

Birds are divided into Orders, as shown on page 16.

In the wall cases of the southern wing on the Upper Floor is the FOREIGN COLLECTION OF BIRDS; but for want of space it is not arranged in its respective orders.

Order ACCIPITRES. There is a splendid collection from all parts of the world of birds belonging to this order, but in consequence of the large amount of space required for its exhibit, it is partly arranged for the present in the gallery of the "Old Wing." Nearly all the principal families are well represented, from the Condor (*Sarcoramphus grypus*) of the Andes to the smallest Falcon known (*Falco fringillarius*) of Java. Of the nocturnal birds of prey the Eagle-owl (*Bubo maximus*), the Snowy Owl (*Surnia nyctea*), and Long-eared Owl (*Strix otus*) are worthy of attention.

Order PSITTACI. This order is exhibited in Bay No. 2. It includes the varied and richly-plumaged species of Parrots and Cockatoos (*Psittacidæ*). The curious Owl-Parrot or Kakapo (*Strigops habroptilus*) of New Zealand, is worthy of notice.

Order PICARIÆ. This order will be found in the wall cases of Bay No. 3. The most striking are the Orange-backed Woodpecker (*Brachypternus aurantius*) of India, the Yellow-fronted Woodpecker (*Picus flavifrons*) from Brazil, and the Pigmy Woodpecker (*Picumnus minutissimus*) of Bahia; and among the Cuckoos, the brilliant Emerald Cuckoo (*Chrysococcyx smaragdinus*) of South Africa is deserving of special attention.

Order PASSERES, in Bay No. 4 includes the genera *Corvus, Paradisea, Sturnella, Aplonis, Pastor, Ampelis,* and the brilliant plumaged Cock of the Rock (*Rupicola crocea*), *Cotinga, Oriolus,* &c.

In the centre case of Bay 3 will be found the different species of Toucans (*Buceros,*) Finches (*Fringillidæ*), and Tanagers (*Tanagridæ*).

In the wall case of Bay No. 3 is a fine group of Paradise Birds, including the " Rifle," and " Bower-building Birds " from New Guinea.

Order COLUMBÆ are placed in Bay No. 2. The curious Tooth-billed Pigeon (*Didunculus strigirostris*) allied to the extinct Dodo, and the Nicobar Pigeon (*Geophilus nicobaricus*) are worthy of attention.

Order GALLINÆ will be found in Bay No. 1. This includes all the different species of Pheasants, of which the Argus, Golden, Impeyan, and Silver are worthy of notice on account of their striking and varied plumage; there will also be found here Quail, Partridges, Grouse, Peafowl, and many other game birds. In Bay No. 7 will be found the genus Otis, represented by the well known *Otis tarda* of Europe.

Order GRALLATORES are in the floorcase of Bay No. 7, the most conspicuous being the Scarlet Ibis from South America, the Snipe (*Gallinago*), the Rail (*Porzana*), and the Parra (*Parra gallinacea*); and in Bay No. 8, the Pratincole (*Glareola*), Bittern (*Butoroides*).

E

Order **NATATORES** are in Bay No. 6. The principal genera exhibited are :—The Albatross (*Diomedea*), the Gulls (*Larus*), the Terns (*Sterna*), and the Cormorant (*Graculus*). In the floor case of this Bay will be found the different species of Ducks (*Anatidæ*) and Grebes (*Podicipedidae*). Bay No. 7 also contains Swimming Birds, principally Ducks, Swans and Geese.

Order **STRUTHIONES** are in Bay No. 5, the principal species represented being the Cassowaries (*Casuarius*) from Queensland and New Guinea, and the *Apteryx* representing the Wingless Birds from New Zealand ; a very fine albino specimen of the latter genus will be found with others.

VII.

AUSTRALIAN BIRDS.

THE upper floor of the north wing contains the collection of Australian birds. Altogether, there are about 760 species found in Australia and the adjacent islands, of which nearly 700 are represented in the Museum. Our avi-fauna possesses some curious genera, such as *Menura, Ptilonorhynchus, Chlamydodera, Scenopœus, Leipoa, Talegallus, Pedionomus,* and others. For beauty and striking contrasts of plumage, the birds of Australia are unrivalled, and the idea that they have no note or song is without foundation. In the Australian Bush, what is more pleasant than to listen in the early morning to the flute-like notes of the piping Crow-shrike (*Gymnorhina tibicen*) and the rich and varied natural notes of the Lyre-bird (*Menura superba*), far excelling those of the Song-thrush, and having immense powers of mimicry and ventriloquism. This power of ventriloquism is also possessed by the Atrichias, and the Oreoica, while the cheerful notes of the Robins, Flycatchers, and many others of the smaller birds testify to the fact that our birds have both a pleasing note and varied song.

On entering the northern wing the first thing to arrest attention is a large case containing two groups of Lyre-birds (*Menura superba*). On the left hand side is a nest containing the young bird, with the male and female close at hand. On the other side is a nest in which the single egg laid by this bird for a sitting is shown. Two adult birds, male and female, complete the group. A very good representation is given of the localities which these birds love to frequent and of their breeding places.

To the right of the above case is another (No. 86), containing a group of Mortier's Tribonyx (*Tribonyx mortieri*), ten in all, showing the different stages of plumage, from the young just out of the shell to the fully adult stage. A very good idea of the habits of these birds is given by the representation of a rush-bordered stream. On the left-hand side of the group of Lyre-birds

is a case containing several of the curious Bower-building
Birds, the Satin Bower-bird (*Ptilonorhynchus violaceus*), and a
bower or playing-ground constructed by them. The bower is
composed of small sticks, twigs, &c., stuck upright in the ground,
surrounded by a platform of sticks, and ornamented with land
shells, bones of small animals, feathers, &c. These bowers
are usually constructed beneath the lower undergrowth in thickly
timbered mountainous parts of the country, and when near the
settlers' houses are often ornamented with pieces of broken
china, glass, &c. The bower must not be confounded with the
nest, which is built in the fork of a tree not far from the ground.
This case contains two adult males, three females, and one
immature male, the latter showing a mixture of the violet-black
and greyish-green stage of plumage. Close at hand is a group
of another species of Bower birds (*Chlamydodera cerviniventris*),
the Fawn-breasted Bower bird of Cape York, and New Guinea.
The bower of this bird is longer, thicker, and more closely
constructed than that of the Satin Bower bird. This is the only
species of the genus *Chlamydodera* that has not the beautiful
rose-coloured frill on the nape of the neck. In the central
portion of the northern wing is Case No. 88, containing several
groups of birds, among which are the Eastern Bower-bird
(*Chlamydodera orientalis*), the Rifle-bird (*Ptilorhis paradisea*), the
Regent-bird (*Sericulus melinus*), with its gay and striking contrasts of golden and velvety black plumage; the Cat-bird
(*Ailurœdus viridis*), so called on account of its harsh and extraordinary notes, resembling the cries of a cat; and on the rockwork
at the bottom of the case is a group of Noisy Pittas (*Pitta
strepitans*). At the back of this case is another containing Prince
Albert's Lyre-bird (*Menura alberti*) adult male and female;
also, the nest hidden by a projecting fern-covered bank. Midway
down the centre of the main hall is a large case, containing a
group of Cassowaries (*Casuarius australis*) from the dense scrubs
of North-eastern Queensland; this bird almost equals the Emu
in size and weight of body. This is the last of the groups in
separate cases.

On each side of the northern wing of the Museum are wall
cases, from which others spring at right angles at various intervals,

forming bays, in which the birds will be found arranged in their respective orders. Returning to the south-western portion of the northern wing, or left-hand side, will be found the first order.

Order ACCIPITRES. Every known species on the Australian continent is here represented. In the first Bay is a group of Wedge-tailed Eagles (*Aquila audax*), and the White-bellied Sea Eagle (*Haliaëtus leucogaster*). These birds are almost equal in size, and are the largest of all the Australian Birds of Prey. The Whistling Eagle (*Haliastur sphenurus*) is also in this case. In the centre of this bay, in the wall case, is a collection of Hawks, Harriers, Kestrels, &c., the most conspicuous of them being the Grey-backed, or New-Holland Goshawk (*Astur cinereus*), the Tasmanian Goshawk (*Astur novæ-hollandiæ*), the former of which in the male has snow-white plumage, and in the female an ashy-grey back; but in the latter both sexes are white. Both species are found in Australia, but the latter form appears to be confined to Tasmania. The Black-shouldered Kite (*Elanus axillaris*), the Nankeen Kestrel (*Tinnunculus cenchroides*), the Collared Sparrow Hawk (*Accipiter cirrhocephalus*), the Black Falcon (*Falco subniger*), and the Black-breasted Buzzard (*Gypoictinia melanosternon*), are all deserving of careful examination. On the right-hand side of this bay will be found the White-headed Osprey (*Pandion leucocephalus*), the Crested Hawk (*Baza subcristata*), the Red-backed Fish-Eagle (*Haliastur girrenera*, a sub-species of *H. indus*), the Brown Hawk (*Hieracidea orientalis*), and the commonest of all our Australian birds of prey. On the lower portion of this case are several specimens of the Powerful Owl (*Ninox strenua*). On entering bay No. 2, other members of the family will be found, among which may be pointed out the Winking Owl (*Ninox connivens*), and the Boobook Owl (*Ninox boobook*).

Order PSITTACI are exhibited in Bay No. 4. This Order is well represented in Australia, from the Great Palm Cockatoo, (*Microglossus aterrimus*) to the Little Lorikeet (*Trichoglossus pusillus*) ; the Cockatoos (*Calyptorhynchus* and *Cacatua*), are interesting forms, but for brilliancy of plumage the Red-winged Lory (*Ptistes erythropterus*), Barraband's Parrakeet (*Polytelis barrabandi*), Banded Parrakeet (*Platycercus zonarius*), and many others surpass the larger and noisier members of the family *Psittacidæ*. The others most worthy of attention, are the Beautiful Parrakeet (*Psephotus pulcherrimus*), Elegant Grass-Parrakeet (*Euphema elegans*) Bourke's Grass-Parrakeet (*Euphema bourkii*) and the Porphyry-crowned Lorikeet (*Trichoglossus porphyrocephalus*). In the right hand corner at the bottom of this case is a group consisting of the male and female Ground Parrakeet (*Pezoporus formosus*), together with the nest and eggs. This species and an allied form found in Western Australia are the only Australian members of the family known to make nests of grass or rushes on the ground, as all the rest resort to the hollow limbs of trees usually at a great height from the ground for the purpose of breeding.

Order **PICARIÆ.** At the top of the case, in Bay 2, are several representative families of the CAPRIMULGIDÆ, including *Ægotheles*, *Caprimulgus*, *Eurostopodus*, and *Podargus*. Attention should be given to the Tawny-shouldered Podargus (*Podargus strigoides*), better known to many under the erroneous local name of " More pork,"—the bird which utters the peculiar note resembling these words being the Boobook Owl; also to the smallest bird of the family, the Owlet Nightjar (*Ægotheles novæ-hollandiæ*). The Dollar Bird (*Eurystomus pacificus*), the Bee-eater (*Merops ornatus*), and the different species of King-fishers belonging to the genera *Dacelo*, *Halcyon*, *Alcyone* and *Tanysiptera* will be found in the same case. On the bottom of this case are the various species of Cuckoos found in Australia.

Order **PASSERES,** are in the wall case of Bay No. 2. This is the largest order of birds in Australia and only a cursory glance can be bestowed on the leading families. The family HIRUNDINIDÆ comprises several graceful genera in the Swallows, and Martins; a pure white or albino specimen of the Fairy Martin, (*Lagenoplastes ariel*) will be found in this case, and at the bottom of it are the Wood Swallows (*Artamidæ*). A faithful representation is given of the position in which the Diamond Bird (*Pardalotus punctatus*), forms its burrow, at the end of which it constructs its nest of loosely interwoven strips of bark or grasses; members of the same family will be found in close proximity. On the right hand side of the Bay are different species of the genera *Strepera*, *Gymnorhina*, and *Grallina*; albino specimens of the two latter are exhibited. Lower down are members of the genus *Graucalus*, and the Flycatchers, representing the genera *Rhipidura*, *Saulo-procta*, *Piezorhynchus*, *Monarcha*, and *Machærirhynchus*, of which the White-shafted-Fantail (*Rhipidura albiscapa*), calls for special attention on account of its curiously formed nest, which may be seen in one of the table cases. The Coach-whip-bird (*Psophodes crepitans*), Noisy scrub bird (*Atrichia clamosa*), Crested Wedge Bill (*Sphenostoma cristatum*), and the numerous members of the genus *Sericornis*, are worthy of attention. At the bottom of this case will be seen a group consisting of the male, female, and nest of the Downy Pycnoptilus (*Pycnoptilus floccosus*). It is only during the last few years that this bird has been found within fifty miles of Sydney; it is a lover of the dense thickets and scrubs of the Illawarra and Blue Mountain ranges. Specimens of *Menura alberti*, and *M. superba*, are also shown. At the top of bay No. 3 on the left hand side are the Crow-Shrikes belonging to the genera *Cracticus* and *Gymnorhina*, lower down are the Thickheads (*Pachycephala*), Collyriocinclæ, and Crested Oreoica (*Oreoica cristata*), the Scarlet-breasted or Legge's Robin (*Petroica leggii*), Red-capped Robin (*P. goodenovii*), Rose-breasted Robin (*Erythrodryas rosea*), and several species of Yellow Robins (*Eopsaltriæ*), the Superb Warblers (*Maluri*), and the curious little Emu Wren (*Stipiturus malachurus*); on the bottom of this case are the Ephthianuræ, one of them, the Orange-fronted (*E. aurifrons*), represented with its nest and eggs, a group of the Australian Meadow Pipit (*Anthus australis*), the White-faced Xerophila (*X. leucopsis*), the Field Calamanthus (*C. campestris*), and the Bristle-bird (*Sphenura brachyptera*). At the back of the bay or wall case on the top row will be found, with but few exceptions, all the members of the family *Ploceidæ* known in Australia. Many of these are very gay plumaged birds, notably the Beautiful Grass Finch (*Poëphila mirabilis*), the Crimson Finch (*Estrilda phäeton*), and the Painted Finch (*Emblema picta*); on the second row are the Pittas and Ground Thrushes, the different species of Bower-building birds (*Scenopœidae*), and groups of Cat Birds (*Ailurœdus viridis*, and *A. maculosus*), and the curious Tooth-billed Scenopœus (*Scenopœus dentirostris*), which has a habit

of clearing a space of ground in the scrub, and ornamenting
it with gaily tinted leaves, flowers and bright berries. The
Regent Bird (*Sericulus melinus*) is also shown with its bower. A
very good idea of the breeding places of the Rock Warbler
(*Origma rubricata*) is given, a group of these birds being set up
with their long pensile nests attached to an overhanging rock.
Close by is a group of Noisy Pittas (*Pitta strepitans*) showing
their manner of obtaining food by breaking shells against a stone,
in time accumulating thereby a large heap of broken shells. On
the right hand side of this bay we come to the largest family
of birds in Australia—the *Meliphagidæ* or Honey-eaters; these
birds procure their food from various native flowers, principally
the *Eucalypti*, their brush-like tongue being well suited for the
purpose; the family consists of many genera, the principal of
which are *Meliornis*, *Glyciphila*, *Ptilotis*, *Philemon*, *Myzomela*,
Melithreptus, and *Myzantha*, the different species of which are
well represented in the collection.

Order COLUMBÆ. Crossing to the eastern side of the
northern wing, we find in Bay No. 5 the order Columbæ or
Pigeons, many of which are of bright colours, especially the
Ptilinopi or Fruit-eating Pigeons. The Bronze-wing (*Phaps
chalcoptera*), the Wonga Wonga (*Leucosarcia picata*), and the
Partridge Bronze-wing (*Geophaps scripta*), are worthy of notice,
and many of them are esteemed great delicacies for the table.

Order GALLINÆ. At the bottom of the case in Bay
No. 5 are several families representing the order Gallinae the
principal of which are the *Perdicidæ* or Quails; these birds
afford good sport in the season, and are much sought after,
especially the Stubble Quail (*Coturnix pectoralis*), and the
Varied Turnix or Painted Quail (*Turnix varius*), two of the
largest species of the family in New South Wales. The
Collared Plain-wanderer (*Pedionomus torquatus*)* a most interesting form and peculiar to Australia is also represented.
At the top of the floor case of this Bay are the Mound-raisers,
a group of birds which deposit their eggs in large mounds of

---

* There is some doubt to which order this bird belongs, some orni-
thologists preferring to place it among the Grallatores.

leaves, debris, and sand, scraped together by the birds, the heat from which while decomposing relieves the parent birds of all further responsibility as regards their incubation. The Mound-raising Megapode (*Megapodius tumulus*) and the Wattled Tale-gallus (*Talegallus lathami*) are found in the rich brushes of the Northern and Eastern coast of Australia, while the Ocellated Leipoa (*Leipoa ocellata*) gives preference to the Mallee scrubs of the interior.

Order GRALLATORES.
The Order Grallatores comes next in Bay No. 6, and includes many genera; several groups are shown, one of them being the Australian Bustard (*Eupodotis australis*), which is worthy of attention as being the largest of all our game birds. Among the Wading Birds the most interesting are the Red-headed Avocet *(Recurvirostra rubricollis)*, the Banded Stilt *(Cladorhynchus pectoralis)*, and the White-headed Stilt (*Himantopus leucocephalus*). In this bay will be found also the different species of Water Crakes, Ibises, Dotterels, Gallinules, Spoonbills, Herons, Bitterns, &c.

Order NATATORES.
The species representing this order are in Bay No. 7. These are the Ducks, Geese, Grebes, &c., and the large and varied species of sea birds found frequenting the seas that wash the Australian coast; among these may be pointed out the different species of Albatross, Gulls, Petrels and Cormorants. In this bay is a group of the Red-tailed Tropic Bird *(Phäeton rubricauda)*, representing the breeding place with an egg of the species.

Order STRUTHIONES or Running Birds.
We now come to the last of the Australian Birds, which for want of space are placed in Bay No. 8, viz., a group of Emus (*Dromaius novæ-hollandiæ*) with their eggs and young. It is a matter of regret that this fine bird is being so rapidly exterminated, and that in a few years, the only examples likely to be met with will be from the interior of Australia.

VIII.

REPTILIA AND BATRACHIA.

THE REPTILES and the BATRACHIANS have so many characteristics in common that it is convenient to study them side by side, although the modern system of classification does not group them together.

REPTILES include snakes, lizards, tortoises, turtles, crocodiles, and alligators ; they are air-breathing animals, with large lungs and cold blood.

BATRACHIANS differ from reptiles in having the skull united to the backbone by *two* joints or condyles, while reptiles have only one, and by having no scales. Most of the Batrachians have four limbs like the higher animals. They lay eggs and have cold blood. The Batrachians consist of animals which during the early stage of their development undergo a complete metamorphosis, living in water and breathing like fishes by means of gills, which in the adult state disappear and are replaced by lungs, while at the same time the tail, in the greater number of forms, is shed, and four limbs are developed.

Reptiles and Batrachians are divided into orders as on page 16.

REPTILIA—Order I.—CHELONIA.—The Tortoises and Turtles which form this order are the only reptiles which have not distinctly elongated bodies. They are protected by a hard bony outer skeleton, technically known as the exo-skeleton, formed of horny plates. The vertebræ are united, making the backbone practically one straight bone. They have no teeth, these being replaced by a horny beak. The head, limbs, and tail protrude from openings in the carapace, and can, in most species be withdrawn at will. In the Central Hall, upper floor, are specimens shewing the formation of the skeleton, and the following mounted examples :—

The **Murray River**, or Long-necked **Tortoises** (*Chelodina longicollis* and *C. oblonga.*)

Sphargis coriacea, from Newcastle, N.S.W. and E. Australia.

Carettochelys insculptus, *(Ramsay)*, a new remarkable form from New Guinea.

Chelonia squamata, from Northern Australia.

Order II.—CROCODILIA.—The Crocodiles, Alligators and Caymans inhabit both the fresh and salt waters of tropical countries, and are the largest reptiles now existing, having been known to grow to 25 feet in length. They have a fully developed backbone and ribs and four limbs, the hind pair being fully webbed; the outer covering consists of horny scales, with soft skin interposed.

Crocodiles have one tooth on each side of the lower jaw longer than the others, so that it is seen outside when the mouth is shut; and the hind feet are webbed. Alligators do not show the long tooth when the mouth is closed, and the hind feet are only partially webbed. Specimens are shown in the Central Hall, Upper Floor, and skeletons in a case in the Osteological Hall, Ground Floor. Crocodiles are found in Africa, India, North Australia, South and Central America. Alligators are found only in the warmer parts of North and South America.

The Australian species are—

Crocodilus porosus.

    „   **johnstonii.**

Order III.—LACERTILIA, or LIZARDS.—In general appearance these reptiles are well known. The four limbs are usually well developed, but in some snake-like forms they are rudimentary. The teeth are not set in sockets in the jaws, but are often united to the bone. The skin is covered with scales. The backbone is composed of many vertebræ, and there is usually a long tail. The Lizards are not poisonous, with one exception —the *Heloderma* of Mexico and Arizona—which has a poison gland and fangs in its upper jaw, and whose bite is occasionally fatal even to man.

There are many families of Lizards, distinguished mainly by the form of the feet, the former being either furnished with disk-like plates (as in the *Geckonidæ*) which enable their owners to pursue their insect prey on walls and even ceilings, with well developed clawed toes (as in the *Agamidæ*) or with rudimentary feet (as in the *Pygopodidæ*). In some the tongue is long, slender or worm-like, in others it is short and fleshy.

The specimens of Australian Lizards are shown in Case 15*b* in the Australian Hall, Ground Floor. Some of them worthy of note are :—

Gymnodactylus platurus—The Gecko, a very harmless little lizard.

Pygopus lepidopus—A Snake-like Lizard.

Amphibolurus barbatus—The Bearded Lizard.

Moloch horridus—Spined Lizard, a purely Australian form.

Varanus varius—The Australian Iguana or Lace Lizard, but the name Iguana is a misnomer, the true Iguanas being American.

Trachysaurus rugosus—The Stump-tailed Lizard.

Tiliqua scincoides—The blue-tongued Lizard.

Lygosoma tæniolatum—The common striated Lizard.

Order IV.—OPHIDIA, or SNAKES.—The Snakes have a terrible fascination, on account of the dangerous venom possessed by many. They possess an internal skeleton composed of very numerous vertebræ, and an external covering of horny scales, which they cast at intervals, during which time they are partially blind ; some serpents, notably the Boas and Pythons, have as many as 400 vertebræ. The lower jaw is united to the upper by muscles only, and even the two sides of the lower jaw are loose, so that they are able to open their mouth to an enormous extent. The teeth are not set in sockets, as they are not used for mastication, but only for siezing the prey. Snakes have no feet, but the backbone and ribs are very flexible, and the locomotion is effected by means of the latter. The tongue is forked, and is a very sensitive organ of touch ; often it is considered by persons with no scientific knowledge, to be the agent by which the poison is introduced into the system, but the poison glands lie at the root of a pair of fangs, one on each side of the upper jaw, and the poison is ejected through a groove in the tooth. The poisonous snakes have few teeth, while the non-poisonous have many. Australian snakes are in Case 15a Australian Hall. Foreign Snakes are in a Case in the Central Hall.

Snakes are divided into the following sub-orders* :—

Sub-order I. SOLONOGLYPHA, which includes Vipers and Rattlesnakes.

—These have broad, flat, triangular heads, with one large moveable fang and a poison gland. The common adder or viper of Europe, the vipers of Africa, the puff adder of South Africa, and other similar snakes form one family of this sub-order. Another family is composed of the rattlesnake of America and similar species.

Sub-order II. PROTEROGLYPHA.

—This sub-order includes some of the most deadly of all snakes, and is well represented in Australia. Its peculiarity is that the poison fangs are grooved in front and are not movable, while behind the fangs are one or more teeth. It is divided into two families.

1. The *Elapidæ*, which have a very broad head. The Cobra (*Naja tripudians*) of India, and the Speckled Snake (*Naja haje*) of Egypt belong to this family, as also the Hamadryad or Tree Snake of India, and others. The principal Australian forms are :—

Acanthophis antarctica—Death Adder.

Hoplocephalus curtus—Brown-banded Snake.

    „   **variegatus**—Broad-headed Snake.

    „   **coronoides**—Tasmanian Snake.

    „   **signatus**—Black-bellied Snake.

Diemenia superciliosa—Brown Snake.

    „   **reticulata**—Whip Snake.

---

* This classification is from Nicholson's Zoology. 7th ed. 1887.

Pseudechis porphyriacus—Black Snake, and the most common of the larger venomous snakes of Australia.

Brachysoma diadema—Scarlet-spotted Snake, which seldom grows over a foot and a half in length.

Tropidechis carinata—Keeled-scaled Snake.

Vermicella annulata—Ringed Snake.

Pseudonaja nuchalis—Collared Snake.

2. The *Hydrophidæ*, or Sea Snakes.—These are all venomous, and are distinguished from land snakes by the formation of the tail, which is flattened for swimming. They are air-breathing animals, although living in the water, and the nostrils are on the top of the snout. Three species found about Port Jackson are :—

Pelamis bicolor—Yellow-bellied Sea Snake.

Platurus scutatus—Ringed Sea Snake.

Hydrophis elegans—Elegant Sea Snake.

Sub-order III.—OPISTHOGLYPHA. In this sub-order the head is long, the fangs are *behind*, and there are several teeth in front. It is not certain whether they are poisonous or not. The American whipsnakes belong to this sub-order, but they are not found in Australia.

Sub-order IV.—AGLYPHODORTA. The snakes of this order are not poisonous; they have no grooved fangs, but have numerous teeth. This order includes the Pythons or Rock snakes, of which the Boa Constrictor is a notable example. Australian specimens are :—

Morelia spilotes—Diamond Snake.

    ,,   **variegata**—Carpet Snake.

Aspidiotes ramsayi—Rock snake, which grows to a length of 20ft., and is one of the largest snakes in Australia.

Liasis childreni—Rock Snake.

Dendrophis punctulata—Green Tree Snake.

Dipsas fusca—Brown Tree Snake.

Nardoa gilberti—Gilbert's Rock Snake.

Sub-order V.—ANGIOSTOMATA. This group contains a number of small snakes not included in any of the preceding groups. The mouth is narrow, and the jaws are not so moveable as in other orders. In some species teeth are wanting. Australian specimens are:—

Typhlops nigrescens—Blind Snake.
    „   **rueppelli**—   „
    „   **guentheri**—   „

They live principally in the ground on minute ants and their eggs. They can really see as well as any other snakes.

BATRACHIA—Sub-Order I.—BATRACHIA SALIENTIA.—This sub-order comprises Batrachians, such as Frogs and Toads, the members of which in the adult state are tail-less, but are provided with four well developed limbs. Specimens of those belonging to Australia and the South Sea Islands are in Case 15b in the Australian Hall, Ground Floor. Some of the species on view are:—

Hyla cærulea—Green Tree Frog.
    „   **aurea**—   „

Notaden bennetti—Bennett's Toad, a very rare and purely Australian form.

Limnodynastes peronii—Marsh frog.

Pseudophryne australis—Speckled bellied frog.

Sub-Order II.—BATRACHIA GRADIENTIA. This sub-order includes Batrachia which retain their tails through life and have also four limbs; while many lead an aquatic life,—for example, the Newts, the Salamanders, the Axolotls, &c., of which there are no Australian examples.

Sub-Order III.—BATRACHIA APODA, or CŒCILIANS.—This Sub-order is characterised by the habits of the animals composing it being serpent or worm-like, having no limbs and only a rudimentary tail—for example, "Mud Eels." They live in marshy ground in tropical countries, but are not found in Australia.

IX.

FISHES.

THESE are the lowest recognized forms of vertebrated animals. The earliest known—and now for the greater part extinct—forms had a cartilagenous skeleton, that is to say the bones, even in the adult state, were represented by a substance resembling "gristle," but many of the later, and sometimes extinct groups, dating back as far as the cretaceous period, are true Teleosteans, which implies that they possess a bony skeleton and completely formed vertebræ, and to this highly specialized sub-class the greater number of recent fishes belong; they are cold-blooded animals, destitute of lungs, which are replaced by gills, a character whose permanency constitutes the chief difference between this and the preceding class. Most fishes are oviparous, but a few genera are ovo-viviparous. The majority of the genera are provided with a scaly covering to the epidermis, as in *Perca*, but in some the skin is absolutely naked, as in *Conger*, while a few of the older forms are protected by bony scutes, as in the Ganoids, and some recent genera have a hard continuous carapace, as shewn in *Ostracion* and *Aracana*. They are almost always wholly aquatic, a few species only being able to exist for a time under other conditions; that certain genera can sustain life out of their natural element has, however, been long known; for example we may mention, (1.) the "Climbing Perch" *Anabas*, of India, which is not only able to leave the water, but by means of its strongly denticulated opercles has been known to climb the sloping sides of trees to a height of several feet, presumably for the purpose of feeding on the insects concealed in the crevices of the bark; (2.) the Eel (*Anguilla*) which migrates over land from place to place in search of water, and has also been proved to make nightly excursions over the meadows adjoining its haunts; (3.) many fishes in tropical climates where the supply of water is precarious, are accustomed to bury themselves in sand or mud on the approach of drought, and are able to survive thus for many months, when rain comes they emerge in great numbers, which accounts for the so-called "showers" of fishes frequently reported in the newspapers. (4.) the Queensland "Mud-hopper" or "Climbing Fish" (*Periophthalmus*) which leaves the water, progressing in advance of the flowing tide by a series of leaps, and even ascends the mangrove trees; many other instances might be adduced but the above are sufficient for our purpose.

Fishes, although living almost entirely under water, breathe oxygen, which they obtain from the water by means of their gills; and although nearly all fishes are oviparous, some hatch out the eggs inside the body (*Cristiceps, Mustelus, &c.*); others in a sub-caudal pouch (*Syngnathus, &c.*); others again in the mouth of the male parent (*Hemipimelodus, &c.*)

Fishes are the oldest recognised types of vertebrate animals, remains having been found in the Upper Silurian strata, near Ludlow. They are classified as on pages 16 and 17.

The first sub-class, the **PALÆICHTHYES**, has been sub-divided into two orders (i.) the *Chondropterygii*, including Sharks, Rays, and Chimæras, and (ii.) the *Ganoidei*, which latter are but little represented in recent times though at one time they existed in large numbers.

Order CHONDROPTERYGYII.

The principal families of this order are (1) the *Carchariidæ*, to which belong such formidable creatures as the Blue Shark (*Carcharias glaucus*), the Whaler (*C. macrurus*), the Tiger Shark (*Galeocerdo rayneri*), and the Hammer-head (*Sphyrna zygæna*), with many smaller forms; (2) the *Lamnidæ*, containing the no less formidable Blue and White Pointers (*Lamna glauca* and *Carcharodon rondeletii*), the Grey Nurse (*Odontaspis taurus*), the curious Fox Shark or Thresher (*Alopias vulpes*), and the still more curious Basking Shark (*Cetorhinus maximus*), which grows to over thirty feet in length, but is quite harmless; (3) the *Heterodontidæ*, to which belong the Port Jackson or Bull-head Sharks (*Heterodontus phillipi* and *H. galeatus*), and which is interesting on account of its great

F

age in point of time, this being the only surviving genus out of
the twenty-five which have been described from remote eras of the
earth's history; (4) the *Spinacidæ* of which two very curious forms
Centrina salviani and *Echinorhinus spinosus* are exhibited in Case
16b; (5) the *Pristiophoridæ* and (6) the *Pristidæ* bear a strong
outward resemblance to one another, but the former are true
Sharks, the latter true Rays; (7) the *Torpedinidæ*, or "Electric
Rays," of which our common "Numb-fish" (*Hypnos subnigrum*)
is a good example, and whose battery is sufficiently powerful to
give a most unpleasant shock; (8) the *Trygonidæ* or "Sting-
Rays" armed with a strong serrated spine on the tail, with which
they can inflict a severe, and in some cases, dangerous wound.
Numerous species are found on our coast, the "Black Sting-
Ray" (*Trygon pastinaca*) being the largest, (9) the *Myliobatidæ*
or "Eagle Rays," some genera of which grow to an enormous
size, even as much as fifteen feet in breath, and attain to a weight
of 1,500 pounds; *Ceratoptera alfredi* in the Central Hall, Upper
Floor, will give a good idea of this family; (10) the *Chimæridæ*, a
small but interesting family representing the sub-order *Holocephala*
and forming a connecting link between the *Chondropterygii* and
Ganoidei; *Callorhynchus antarcticus*, the "Elephant-fish," of
Bass' Straits, is the only Australian representative; the exhibits
belonging to this order are placed in Cases 13a, 13b (mounted
and in spirits), while Case 12 in the Osteological Hall contains
skeletons; the large mounted species are hung round the Central
Hall, Upper floor. Other families represented in the Museum
are (11) *Notidanidæ*, Seven-gilled shark; (12) *Scylliidæ*, Dog-
fishes; (13) *Rhinidæ*, Monk or Angel fish; (14) *Rhinobatidæ*,
Shovel-nosed, and Fiddler Rays, and (15) *Raiidæ*, true Rays or
Skates.

Order GANOIDEI.—Of this order, a fairly representative
series is on exhibit, six of the eleven living genera being on view
in Case 13a. These are as follows: Families (1) *Sirenidæ*, represented by *Protopterus annectens* from Tropical Africa, and
Ceratodus forsteri, the only Australian representative of this almost
extinct order; (2) *Acipenseridæ*, by the Sturgeons, natives of the
northern hemisphere, and valuable commercially as affording the
best quality of isinglass and caviare; (3) *Polyodontidæ*, by *Polyodon*

folium, from the Mississippi, remarkable for the great length of its spoon-shaped upper jaw ; (4) *Polypteridæ,* by *Polypterus bichir,* from Tropical Africa, and (5) *Lepidosteidæ* by *Lepidosteus osseus,* and *L. viridis,* the "Bony Pikes" of the southern states of North America.

We now come to the second sub-class, the TELEOSTEI, having a bony skeleton with completely formed vertebræ ; the greater number of recent fishes belong to this sub-class, and they comprise an almost infinite variety of forms. They are divided into six orders.

Order ACANTHOPTERYGII is so named on account of a portion of the dorsal, anal and ventral fins being formed of spines ; the pharyngeal bones, as the fifth branchial arch is called, are generally separate. The principal families are as follows : (1) *Percidæ,* represented by numerous genera and species in the rivers and seas of Australia. The following forms will be familiar to our readers : the English Perch (*Perca*), found commonly over the temperate region of the Northern Hemisphere, and introduced n many parts of the colonies ; the Australian Perch (*Percalates*) ; the Black Rock Cod (*Serranus*), so justly esteemed for the excellence of its flesh; the Pearl Perch (*Glaucosoma*), an even better fish ; the Golden Perch (*Ctenolates*), Silver Bream (*Therapon*), and Murray Cod (*Oligorus*) the last three abundant in our inland waters, and of excellent flavor, and many others ; (2) the *Chætodontidæ,* or "Coral fishes", consisting chiefly of small fishes of exquisite colors ; but one species, the Sweep (*Scorpis*) is marketable ; (3) the *Mullidæ,* or Red Mullets, highly esteemed as they always have been in Europe for the quality of their food, are of little value here ; (4) the *Sparidæ,* or Sea-Breams, are a valuable group in our waters, as the Black-fishes (*Girella*), the Schnapper (*Pagrus*), the Black Bream and Tarwhine (*Chrysophrys*), with several others, belong to it ; (5) the *Cirrhitidæ* contains some of our best table-fish, such as the Jackass-fish (*Chilodactylus*) and the Trumpeters (*Latris*) ; (6) the *Scorpænidæ,* embracing the Red Rock Cods, and many other curious forms ; (7) the *Berycidæ,* which is an interesting family, since to it belong the oldest known Teleostean Fishes, many of its members occurring in the chalk formations, whence several species of *Beryx* have been described, a genus to which our well-known Nannygai belongs; (8.) the *Sciænidæ*, another valuable family to which the Jew-fish (*Sciæna*), and the Teraglin (*Otolithus*), both large and excellent fishes, belong; (9.) the *Trichiuridæ*, among which may be mentioned the famous Frost-fish of New Zealand (*Lepidopus*), the Hair-tails (*Trichiurus*), and the Barracouta of Tasmania (*Thyrsites*), all of fine quality; (10.) the *Carangidæ* or Horse Mackerels with the Yellowtail and Trevally (*Caranx*), the King-fish and Samson-fish (*Seriola*), the Pilot-fish (*Naucrates*) and the Tailor (*Temnodon*) as representatives. (11) *Scombridæ*, or the Mackerels, which includes besides the typical species, a Tunny (*Orcynus*), and species of *Cybium* and *Elacate*, the latter being found in all tropical seas, and the Sucking-fishes (*Echeneis*) with their first dorsal fin transformed into a lamellated sucking disk on the top of the head; (12) *Trachinidæ*, the best known of which to our readers will be the Whitings (*Sillago*) a very delicate morsel; (13) the *Cottidæ*, containing the Flat-heads (*Platycephalus*), and the Gurnards (*Trigla* and *Lepidotrigla*) both of good flavour and the latter with beautifully marked fins; (14) *Blenniidæ*, mostly small fishes of no commercial value, but interesting on account of several of the genera bringing forth living young, such as *Zoarces, Cristiceps*, &c. and (15) *Mugilidae*, or Grey Mullets, a most important family, from whose members may be selected as representatives, the Sea Mullet (*Mugil dobula*), the Flat-tail Mullet (*M. peronii*), and the Tallygalane (*Myxus elongatus*) of whose excellence no mention is necessary; thirty-six other famliies belong to this order.

Order **PHARYNGOGNATHI** differs from the preceding only in having the lower pharyngeal bones coalesced. Four families only are known, the principal one being the *Labridæ* or Parrot-fishes, of which we have many genera and species, among which may be mentioned the Pig-fish and Blue Groper (*Cossyphus*), the true Parrot-fishes (*Labrichthys*), the Rainbow-fishes (*Coris*), and the Rock-Whitings (*Odax*).

Order **ANACANTHINI** is distinguished by the want of spines in the vertical fins, and by the ventral fins rising from the throat or breast. Five families belong to the Anacanthines,

of which the *Gadidæ* or Cod-fishes, and the *Pleuronectidæ* or Flat-
fishes only need concern us ; the former genus is badly represented
here, the Beardie (*Lotella*) being the only common form, while of
the latter the only marketable kinds are the Flounder (*Pseudo-
rhombus*) and the Sole (*Synaptura*).

Order **PHYSOSTOMI** is distinguished from the preceding
by having the ventral fins rise from the belly ; this is an important order, many of the most valuable fishes of commerce
being included in its numbers. The most noticeable families are
(1) the *Siluridæ* or Cat-fishes, represented by numerous genera, and
distributed over the fresh waters and coasts of the tropical and
temperate zones ; the best known genera in Australia are the
River Cat-fish (*Copidoglanis*) and the Estuary Cat-fish (*Cnido-
glanis*) ; (2) the *Scopelidæ*, mostly deep sea fishes, of which the
Rauning (*Saurus*) and the Sergeant Baker (*Aulopus*) will
suffice as representatives ; (3) the *Cyprinidæ* of which the Carp,
Tench, and Barbel furnish good examples, but of which no species
has yet been proved to be indigenous to Australia, though some
have been introduced ; (4) the *Scombresocidæ*, which include the
Long Tom (*Belone*), the Garfish (*Hemirhamphus*) justly considered one of our most delicate fishes, and the Flying-fish
(*Exocœtus*) ; (5) the *Galaxiidæ*, noticeable for its curious distribution, being found only in the Australian colonies, New
Zealand, and Chili ; (6) the *Salmonidæ*, or Salmon and Trout
family, so successfully introduced into the temperate parts of
Australia and New Zealand, and of which the little *Retropinna*
is our sole native representative ; (7) the *Clupeidæ* or Herrings,
numerous species of which abound in our seas, but for want of
proper nets are not brought to market ; (8) the *Murænidæ*
or Eels, as examples of which we may select the River Eel
(*Anguilla*), the Silver Eel (*Murænesox*), and the Green Eel
(*Muræna*).

Order **LOPHOBRANCHII** or Horse fishes, can be mistaken for no other ; the only family which need be mentioned
is the *Syngnathidæ*, which are peculiar on account of the male
being provided with a sub-caudal pouch into which the eggs
are packed on extrusion from the female, and there hatched

out; many genera frequent our seas, the best known being the
Pipe-fish *(Syngnathus)* and the Sea-horses *(Hippocampus* and
Solenognathus), while the most curious form is the *Phyllopteryx*,
which has its body ornamented with long leaf-like filaments,
resembling the fronds of seaweeds and serving as a disguise.

Order **PLECTOGNATHI**, in which the skeleton is incom-
pletely ossified, and the vertebræ in small numbers; it contains
two families only, (1) the *Sclerodermi*, which includes the File-
fishes *(Balistes)*, the Leather-jackets *(Monacanthus)*, many of which
are excellent eating, and the Box-fishes *(Ostracion)* which are
almost entirely covered by a bony carapace; and (2) the *Gymno-*
dontes, to which belongs the Toados *(Tetrodon)* of which the flesh
of many species is poisonous, the Porcupine-fish *(Dicotylichthys)*,
and the Sun-fishes *(Orthagoriscus)*.

The third sub-class, called **CYCLOSTOMATA** on account of
the mouth being surrounded by a circular lip which forms a
suctorial organ, contains the Lampreys, of which two genera are
found in the colonies, viz. *Mordacia* from Tasmania, and *Geotria*
from South Australia. Both genera, as with *Galaxias*, are found
in Chili.

The fourth and last sub-class, the **LEPTOCARDII** consists of
but one family *Cirrostomi*, and two genera *Branchiostoma* with two
and *Epigonichthys* with one Australian species; they are without
ribs, brain, jaws, or heart, and have, not without justice, been
separated from the true fishes altogether.

Typical specimens of all the genera contained in the Museum,
will be found in Cases 16a, 16b, and 16c in the Australian Hall,
Ground Floor.

X.

MOLLUSCA.

The **MOLLUSCA** constitute one of the principal divisions of the animal kingdom, and include such animals as the Octopus, Cuttle-fish, Squid, Snail, Slug, Whelk, and Oyster.

They may be characterized as soft cold-blooded animals, without distinctly marked external segmental divisions into segments (as in worms); their cerebral ganglia lie above the commencement of the œsophagus, and are connected with the inferior ganglia by nerve chords. The heart consists of two or more chambers, is situated on the dorsal side of the animal, and drives the blood into spaces between the various organs of the body. Only the Cephalopods possess an internal cartilage, but none have a bony skeleton; in the majority this is compensated for by an external hardened shell which forms an outer covering to the animal, and is called the mantle. The mantle either forms a free fold on each side of the body, or is largely attached to the body-wall, as in the Snail, or the Slug, and so gives rise to an air-chamber, which, when its walls are richly supplied with blood, serves as a lung. The ventral surface of Molluscs is produced into the so-called "foot," which is very variously modified. The foot may be more or less hatchet shaped, or curved and capable of serving as a leaping organ, or sole-shaped and adapted for creeping; its margins may be produced into elongated processes, as the so-called arms of the *Octopus*, or of the *Nautilus;* or, as in other Cephalopods, another part of the foot may fold over and form a funnel, through which the water used for respiration is driven outwards, causing the animal to move in the opposite direction—this part of the foot having therefore still the function of an organ of locomotion. By means of their muscular foot, the Razor-shells (*Solenidæ*), burrow in the sand, the Pond Snails (*Limnæidæ*) crawl on aquatic plants, and swim reversed on the surface of the water, the Limpets cling to the rock, and the Cockles and Trigonias take surprising leaps.

The greater number of Mollusca are inhabitants of the sea, some passing their whole life at the surface, frequently many hundreds of miles from land ; others at the bottom of the ocean, from which some have been dredged at a depth of four or five miles from the surface ; many are found in shallow water, and a large number between tide-marks ; rivers and lakes furnish an immense variety of forms ; and others live on land in all situations —on mountains, in valleys, forests, and deserts.

Molluscs are either animal or vegetable feeders, the former preying principally upon other members of their own class. They are classified by naturalists as in the table on pages 17 and 18.

CEPHALOPODA.—This class includes the Octopus, Cuttlefish, Squid, Spirula, and the Paper and Pearly Nautilus.

The body of the animal consists of a muscular sac, in the cavity of which the viscera are placed. In front of the body projects the head, which in species belonging to the two-gilled section of the Class, is surrounded by eight or ten fleshy arms. A wide aperture below the head admits the water to the gills or branchiae, which are situated in the interior of the sac, whilst a short tube, the so-called funnel or siphuncle, projects from the opening of the mantle—the water and various excretions being expelled through this tube, especially an ink-like fluid, which is discharged by all Cephalopods (except *Nautilus*) when disturbed in order to darken the water and enable them to escape from their enemies. The centre of the head, between the base of the arms, is occupied by the mouth, which is armed with two horny or calcareous jaws, similar to the beak of a parrot. Two large eyes are placed on the sides of the head. The arms or feet are more or less elongate, capable of movement in any direction, and, (except in *Nautilus*) are furnished on one side with numerous suckers, by means of which the animal attaches itself most securely to whatever it may seize ; they are employed capturing food and in walking. Cephalopods can walk in any direction head downwards, but can swim backwards only, being propelled in that direction by the water which they discharge with force through the funnel leading from their branchial cavity. They are divided according to the number of their gills, which is either two or four, into *Dibranchiata* and *Tetrabranchiata*. The former breathe by a single pair of internal symmetrical branchiæ or gills. The eyes are sessile. The mandibles are horny. They have eight or ten arms furnished with rows of acetabulæ or suckers. The body is sometimes laterally or posteriorly finned. The shell is either internal or absent. The two-gilled section contains species with eight arms, as *Argonauta* and *Octopus*, and others with ten arms, as the Cuttlefishes (*Sepia*), the Squids (*Loligo, Ommatostrephes*, &c.) and *Spirula*. The "shells," of the Paper Nautilus, (*Argonauta*), are found after strong easterly gales on the outer beaches of the coast at Port Stephens. The shells of *Spirula* are also found scattered on the shores of Bondi and Coogee Bays; a few imperfect ones, containing a portion of the animal, have been obtained on the coast and may be seen in spirits. A number of these specimens are exhibited in a case at the North end of the Upper Floor. Of the latter Section (*Tetrabranchia*) but one representative now exists, viz., the Pearly Nautilus, breathing by two pair of branchiæ, having the mandibles shelly, the arms very numerous and without suckers, the shell external, chambered, and capable of containing the animal.

Three species of the Paper Nautilus (*Argonauta*), the Pearly Nautilus (*Nautilus pompilius*), and four others amongst which is *Spirula peroni*, will be found in Case 1.

PTEROPODA.—The Pteropoda are exhibited in Case 1. They are small molluscs, some of them even microscopic, and are popularly known as "Sea-butterflies" and "Whale food." The first of these names has been given on account of their form and the incessant movements of their swimming lobes; the second because they form a portion of the food of the Balæna and other Whales, as well as of a great number of fishes. The Pteropoda live at a certain depth beneath the surface, and approach the shore only when carried by storms or currents.

Like the preceding group they are organized for swimming freely in the ocean. They progress by means of a pair of fins which are developed from the sides of the mouth or neck, Numerous species are found on the coast at Port Stephens after bad weather, and some have been taken by the towing net in Port Jackson.

GASTROPODA are so termed from the circumstance of their crawling or gliding on the under surface of their body, termed the "foot." They have been divided into four sections:—1. The *Prosobranchiata*, which have the gills situated behind the head in advance of the heart, and are always provided with a shell. 2. The *Opisthobranchiata* in which the position and structure of the gills are variable, but always behind the heart, and in which the body is either naked or protected by a shell, external or concealed in the mantle. 3. The *Nucleobranchiata*, which have the gills in a tuft at the hinder part of the back, in some cases protected by a shell; they do not crawl like the ordinary Gastropods, but are found swimming freely in the open sea, like the Pteropods. 4. The *Pulmonata*, or air-breathers, the breathing-cavity of which opens only by a small aperture which can be closed by a valve. These four primary divisions of Gastropods have been variously split up into smaller sections—families, genera, and subgenera.

PROSOBRANCHIATA.—The family of *Muricidæ*, or "Rock-shells," comprises many of the largest and most beautiful shells hitherto discovered, often remarkable for the delicacy of their sculpture and the variety of their colours. They are all carnivorous, feeding chiefly on other Mollusca, boring through the shells of bivalves with their spiny tongue, and slowly devouring the unfortunate inhabitant piecemeal. From one species found in the Mediterranean (*Murex brandaris*), the ancients manufactured the celebrated Tyrian purple dye: specimens of these are exhibited in the case. The family of *Buccinidæ* contains a very large and various assemblage of forms. Among them may be mentioned the Whelks (*Buccinum*), and the " Purples " (*Purpura*) found between tide marks. *Magilus* is found among the coral-reefs of the Solomon Islands and Mauritius, and has the remarkable habit of lengthening the aperture of its shells into an elongate tube, in order to keep pace with the growth of the coral, and so prevent its being overgrown and killed.

The remaining Familes and Orders have not yet been finally arranged in the Cases, and, in the meantime, a full description of them is not given, but the following list of the contents of the cases will be of interest :—

CASE I.—Besides the Families already described, this case contains the Volutes *(Volutidæ)* a group of shells very much sought after by shell-collectors ; the greatest variety of them are found in Australia.

CASE II.—The Trumpet Shells (*Tritonidæ)* have varices or strengthening ribs at intervals, like the Muricidæ ; the largest species (*Triton tritonis*) is used by the South Sea Islanders, as a horn or trumpet. A hole is sometimes made in the side of the spire to blow through.

CASE III.—The Cowry Shells *(Cypæridæ)* are remarkable for their varied markings and fine polish, which is produced and preserved by two flaps of the mantle, one on each side, which fold over the back, a line down the centre usually marking where the flaps meet. Cowries are sold as orna ments ; the Money Cowry *(C. moneta)* passes current as coin among the negro tribes of Africa and the natives of India. The Orange Cowry (*C. aurantium*) is worn by the chiefs of Viti, or Fiji, and the Friendly Islands, and is considered the highest order of dignity. *C.* (*Trivia*) *australis* is common on the New South Wales coast.

The *Ovulidæ*, the most curious of which, the Weaver's Shuttle, (*Radius volva*), is peculiarly beaked at both ends.

The Helmet Shells (*Cassididæ)* are used for cameo-carving ; they consist of differently coloured layers, so that the ground colour of the carving is of a different tint from the subject engraved.

The Tun Shells (*Doliidæ*) are remarkable for the globose-ness of the shells, which are covered with regular revolving ribs.

CASE IV.—The Mitras *(Mitridæ)* are great favourites with shell-collectors on account of their beautiful colours and varied sculpture. Mitras are mostly found in tropical or sub-tropical regions. Two of the larger forms are *M. episcopalis* and *M. papalis*.

The Wing Shells (*Strombidæ*) are the largest of the Gastropods with a proboscis or non-retractile snout. They do not crawl like most other Gastropods, but progress by a sort of hopping movement. The Scorpion Shells, or Spider Claws as they are sometimes called (*Pterocera*), possess singular claw-like projections, which are developed on the outer lip of the shells.

The Olives (*Olividæ*) are common in most tropical seas, and are remarkable for their beautiful polish and various patterns of colouration. They burrow in sand in quest of bivalves for food, and some species have the power of swimming by expanding the lobes of the foot.

CASE V.—The Harps (*Harpidæ*). The animals inhabiting these beautiful shells are also brightly coloured, and species are known from the Indo-Pacific Ocean.

The Auger Shells (*Terebridæ*) are of elongate shape and have a deep notch at the base of the aperture. Owing to the length and comparative solidity of the shells many of the species do not carry the shelly structures on their backs as most do, but drag them along the sandy bottom.

The Cones (*Conidæ*) form one of the most beautiful families of shells. This group, of which about 500 distinct species are known, is a great favourite with collectors on account of the brilliant colours and varied patterns of the shells. Some, owing to their beauty and rarity, have been sold at very high prices, as much as £50 having been paid for a single shell. The Cones are found in all tropical seas. Four species are found in Port Jackson.

CASE VI.—The *Onustidæ*, including the genera *Phorus* and *Onustus*, have the singular habit of cementing stones, pieces of coral, and fragments of other shells to the exterior of their shell; hence they have been called "carrier-shells," and according to the kind of material chosen, have been named "Conchologists" and "Mineralogists."

The Wentle-traps (*Scalariidæ*), *Naticæ*, the Solariums or Perspective Shells, and Violet Snails (*Ianthinæ*). The Naticas are mostly blind, and have a large foot, suitable for burrowing in sand when in quest of bivalves. There are some fine specimens of *Scalaria pretiosa*, which was formerly considered a great rarity, as much as £50 having been given for a single specimen. The Violet Snails are found floating about in every ocean. They feed upon jelly fish and construct a gelatinous raft filled with air bubbles. A number of varieties are found on the coast of New South Wales.

The Screw-Shells *(Turritellidæ)* have elongate tapering shells, and are found mostly in tropical climates; a few are found on the Australian coast.

The Periwinkles *(Littorinidæ)* are found on every shore; they feed on all kinds of marine vegetation, and numerous species are found in Australia.

The *Cerithiidæ* are chiefly marine forms, some however entering brackish water. Some of the species emit a bright green fluid when molested.

The *Melaniidæ* are fresh water snails; they abound in most tropical and sub-tropical countries. A number of the species are found in Australia.

The River Snails *(Paludinidæ)* might be termed freshwater Periwinkles, as the animals of both are very similar. They are rather sluggish, and are found at bottoms and margins of ponds and rivers, feeding on decaying animal and vegetable matter.

The family of *Calyptræidæ* includes the Slipper Limpets and the Cup-and-Saucer Limpets *(Crucibulum)*.

The Worm Shells *(Vermetidæ)* are a very peculiar family. Their shells can scarcely be distinguished from the shelly tubes, which are formed by certain species of marine worms, *Serpula*, &c. They are free and spiral in early life, but afterwards become distorted and generally attached to rocks, stones, &c.

XI.

INSECTA.

THE perishable nature of the specimens, and their liability to fade when exposed to the light, unfortunately precludes the exhibition of anything approaching a complete collection of this class, but a representative series, showing the more important types of the various orders, is arranged in cases in the Central Hall, Upper Floor. Cases I—III contain Australian species ; while in cases IV and V, a series of Foreign species is exhibited for comparison with the native forms.

The following table, drawn up by Mr. DALLAS, will give some idea of the points of structure which have been made use of in classifying the different families of insects, but it should be used with caution, as it is impossible in a few words to frame a definition which will in every case serve for the discrimination of the Orders :—

I.—INSECTS WITH A PERFECT METAMORPHOSIS.

A. With biting mouths, the jaws always distinct :—

1. Fore-wings horny or leathery, forming a pair of sheaths or cases (elytra), covering the abdomen and hind wings, and generally meeting in a straight line down the middle. 1. *Coleoptera*.

2. All the wings membranous :—
   a. Veins in the wings few; prothorax united with the mesothorax. 2. *Hymenoptera*.
   b. Veins in the wings numerous; prothorax free. 3. *Neuroptera*.

B. With sucking mouths :—

1. Wings four, scaly ; maxillæ forming a spiral proboscis. 4. *Lepidoptera*,

2. Wings not more than two :—
   a. Two wings ; provided with halteres, or balancers ; thoracic segments united ; proboscis formed of the labium, enclosing bristles. 5. *Diptera*.
   b. Wings none ; thoracic segments distinct. 6. *Aphaniptera*.

II.—INSECTS WITH AN IMPERFECT METAMOR-PHOSIS, OR WITH NONE AT ALL.

A. With sucking mouths; rostrum composed of the jointed labium, enclosing bristles. 7. *Rhynchota.*

B. With biting mouths, of which the parts are exposed; no organs of locomotion at the extremity of the abdomen. 8. *Orthoptera.*

C. With biting mouths, the parts of which are usually very delicate, and concealed within the cavity of the mouth ; no wings ; no metamorphosis. 9. *Thysanura.*

AUSTRALIAN INSECTS.

COLEOPTERA, or Beetles, are at once recognisable by having the fore-wings modified into horny coverings, called elytra, which are not used in flight. The mouth-parts are well developed and the transformations or metamorphoses are complete ; they are not, however, so complete as in the Lepidoptera (Butterflies and Moths), the swaddling-cloth of the pupa not forming a simple case, but separately covering body and limbs. The Australian beetles alone have recently been estimated to number more than 30,000 species, of which about 7,300 are actually described, and many more await description in collections.

The *Cicindelidæ* (Tiger-beetles) are represented by about 52 species, including two species of *Megacephala*, and nine of *Tetracha*, genera which find their allies in Africa and South America respectively. The true *Carabidæ* are represented by three species of *Calosoma*, and by the large ground beetles of the genus *Pamborus*, and the other subdivisions by a large number of species, of which those found under bark are especially numerous. Chief among the essentially Australian groups are the *Pseudo-morphinæ*, a curious group of bark beetles, which, although common in Australia, are not represented in New Zealand. The largest known ground beetle, *Hyperion Schrœtteri*, Sc., belonging to the *Morio* group, is not uncommon in certain localities. The following characteristic genera, among many others, are also found :—*Zuphium, Ænigma, Helluo, Pheropsophus, Xanthophœa, Homothes, Sarothrocrepis, Philophlœus, Agonochila, Scopodes, Eutoma, Carenum, Scaraphites, Catadromus.* The true water beetles, *Dytiscidæ*, and the *Hydrophilidæ*, are not very largely represented, and the species, with a few exceptions, are of the ordinary types. The family *Staphylinidæ* (Rove-beetles) contains a large number of mostly minute species. Only a few of them present any marked deviations from the ordinary form. Of these, *Apphiana veris*, Oll., is perhaps the most singular. The *Psephalidæ*, and other families of Clavicorns contain a large number of species, and doubtless many more remain to be discovered. The *Paussidæ*—a remarkable family, of which most of the species are very rare—has nearly fifty Australian representatives. Some of these are known to live in the nests of ants, by whom they are tended with jealousy and care, but very little is known of the exact relationship between them, although it has been maintained, in the case of some species, that they are the unwilling guests of the ants and are forcibly detained by them. Like *Pheropsophus*, and some other genera of Carabidæ, the *Paussi* possess the faculty of crepitation, which is effected by means of anal glands through which they discharge au acrid volatilised liquid; many of our species crepitate loudly when disturbed, and the vapour causes a burning sensation if it comes in contact with the skin. A curious fact in connection with the *Histeridæ* is the apparent absence of the genus *Hister*, a group which, outside Australia, is of world-wide distribution. The *Lucanidæ* contain some remarkable and interesting genera, which afford a striking illustration of the affinity which exists between the fauna of Australia and the west coast of South America. For instance, *Cacostomus* finds its ally in the South American genus *Sphenognathus ; Lissotes* and the Tasmanian *Hoplogonus* approach *Ægognathus ;* and *Neolamprima, Lamprima*, &c., are clearly allied to the Chilian genus *Chiasognathus.*

The *Scarabæid æ* are well represented, the following being the most noticeable genera :—*Cephalodesmus, Tesserodon, Bolboceras, Phyllotocus, Diphucephala, Mæchidius, Liparetrus, Anoplognathus, Cryptodus,* and *Schizorrhina.* The fauna is deficient in the large *Coprinæ*, but we have many small species of *Onthophagus.* The genus *Schizorrhina*, which has recently been divided into numerous sub-divisions, has its head-quarters in Australia. The

Buprestidæ are remarkable for their brilliant colouring. *Stigmodera*, perhaps the most characteristic genus of Australian beetles, contains more than 230 described species.

The *Eucnemidæ* and *Elateridæ* are represented, the latter family in considerable numbers. The Malacoderms include a large number of species belonging to the genera *Metriorrhynchus*, *Telephorus*, *Laius*, *Carphurus*, *Aulicus*, *Eleale*, &c. The large family *Tenebrionidæ* exhibits some very striking forms, such as *Zopherosis*, *Pterohelæus*, *Helæus*, *Saragus*, *Cyphaleus*, *Prophanes*, *Adelium*, *Seirotrana. Amarygmus*, &c. The group Rhynchophora, or weevils, contains more than 1,200 described Australian species, many of them of the most singular forms. The *Amycteridæ*, which in Australia take the place of *Brachycerus* and its allies, a group largely represented in Africa and the Mediterranean region, are commonly found under logs and stones. They appear to be most abundant in the dry parts of the country, but a few species are found in the coast districts of New South Wales. The Longicorns are very numerous, more than 550 Australian species having been described. *Phoracantha*, *Skeletodes*, containing a single species, *Tragocerus*, *Zygocerus*, *Symphyletes*, *Penthea* and *Rhytiphora* are conspicuous genera. The Phytophagous beetles, many of which are destructive to fruit trees and crops, are also very numerous, particularly those of the sub-families *Cryptocephalinæ* and *Chrysomelinæ* One peculiarly Australian genus, *Paropsis*, contains about 270 described forms.

Hymenoptera (Bees, Wasps, Ants, &c.) are characterised by having the first abdominal segment intimately united with the thorax, and the wings, which are of the normal number, with irregular and comparatively few veins. The mouth is mandibular, or formed for biting, and the transformations are complete; many of them have the abdominal appendages modified into a sting. In this order there is a great diversity in the form and habits of the larvæ. Usually they are soft, maggot-like creatures, possessing a corneous or horny head; but in the Saw-flies *(Tenthredinidæ)* the larvæ generally resemble caterpillars, possessing three pairs of true legs, and in the case of those which live on the leaves of plants, several pairs of claspers. Our native honey bees *(Trigona)* are without stings. They live in immense communities, each

G

hive, according to Mr. F. Smith, containing more than one female.
The ordinary hive bee *(Apis mellifica)* is not indigenous, but the
progeny of swarms, which have escaped from captivity, are often
found in a wild state, living in hollow trees or logs in the
most remote parts of the bush. The carpenter bees *(Xylocopa
&c.)* make their nests in wooden posts or tree trunks. *Lestes
bombylans,* Fabr., a beautiful native species, usually makes its nest
in the stems of the grass-tree *(Xanthorrhœa)*. Many kinds
of *Vespidæ*, or wasps, both social and solitary, are found
in Australia. The *Mutillidæ*, a family in which the sexes
differ greatly from each other in many important respects, the
females often being wingless, is largely represented, the most
important genera being *Thynnus* and *Scolia*. The *Formicidæ*,
a family containing the various species of ants, are exceedingly
numerous, and display great diversity in their habits; we
have representatives of nearly all the groups, including the
remarkable honey-ants, of which, besides the ordinary type of
worker, there is a singular form with inflated body, whose sole duty
appears to be the secretion of a peculiar kind of honey. The
Chrysididæ, or so-called golden-wasps, the *Ichneumonidæ*, or
'insect-eaters," the *Proctotrupidæ*, the *Chalcididæ*, and the *Cyni-
pidæ*, or Gall-flies, are all abundant. The *Tenthredinidæ*, or
Saw-flies, include the brightly-coloured species of the genus *Perga*,
a characteristic Australian group.

Neuroptera (Dragon-flies, Caddis-flies, May-flies, &c.) have
ample, thin, net-veined wings, both pairs nearly equal in size,
the mouth-parts free, the mandibles well developed, and the
abdomen long and slender. The transformations are sometimes
complete (true Neuroptera), sometimes incomplete (Pseudo-
Neuroptera). The *Myrmeleontidæ*, or Ant-lions, are, perhaps,
the most interesting forms of this order. The *Ascalaphi*,
Hemerobiidæ, or Lace-wings, and the curious family *Manti-
spidæ*, are also well-known forms. The *Panorpidæ*, represented
by *Bittacus*, &c., and the *Trichoptera*, or Caddis-flies, are well
represented; to the latter group an interesting addition has
recently been made in the shape of a marine species, supposed
to belong to the genus *Phalanisus*, which lives in rock-pools
between tide marks in Port Jackson. The *Termitidæ*, or White-
ants, so well-known for their destructive habits, the *Ephemeridæ*,

or May-flies, and the *Libellulidæ*, or Dragon-flies, also constitute a division of this order.

Lepidoptera, including the Butterflies *(Rhopalocera)* and Moths *(Heterocera)*, are easily distinguished by the scale-covered wings, with regular branching neuration, the small head and highly developed clypeus, or head-shield, and by having the maxillæ modified into a tubular proboscis or tongue. Their transformations are complete, that is they pass through four definite stages of existence—the egg, the caterpillar or larva, the chrysalis or pupa, and the perfect insect or imago. The butterflies are represented in Australia by about 320 known species, by no means a large number when we consider the immense area of the country and the great variety of its climate. However, although this number is small as compared to similar areas in some other parts of the world, as for instance continental India and central and tropical South America, it is in striking contrast to the fauna of New Zealand, which only has 16 representatives, if we except the very doubtful *Hamadryas zoilus,* Fabr. When we remember that in the British Islands there are at least 65 native species, it will be seen that this shows a singular poverty of butterflies. In Australia the *Nymphalidæ, Erycinidæ, Lycænidæ, Papilionidæ,* and *Hesperiidæ,* the five families into which the butterflies are divided, all find a place. The first of these, the *Nymphalidæ,* includes the whole of the great division of butterflies in which the forelegs of the perfect insect are undeveloped, having the foot or tarsus rudimentary in both sexes. It is divided into four sub-families, the *Danainæ, Acræinæ, Nymphalinæ,* and *Satyrinæ.* Eighteen species of *Danainæ* are at present known in Australia, of which *Danais plexippus,* Linn., is an American importation. Our fauna only comprises a single widely distributed member of the *Acræinæ,* but the other two sub-families are represented by about 25 and 34 species respectively. The family *Erycinidæ* is represented in Australia by a single species, *Libythea myrrha,* Godt., which is also found in Borneo, Java, and India. The *Lycænidæ,* a family containing a vast number of species, mostly of small size, has more than 80 representatives. The *Papilionidæ* are represented by about 76 species, of which 52 belong to the sub-family *Pierinæ ;* of the sub-family *Papilioninæ* only a single species, *P. macleayanus,* Le., is found in Tasmania. The *Hesperiidæ*, a family of butterflies which is remarkable for having the chrysalis enclosed in a slight cocoon, or secured by many silken threads, is represented by a large number of species.

Moths are exceedingly numerous. The *Sphingidæ*, or Hawk-moths—the species of which are remarkable for their large size and powerful flight—are represented by about 40 species, many of them finely coloured. Of these *Hemaris hylas*, Linn., one of the "clear-wing" Hawk-moths, and various species of *Macroglossa*, or Humming-bird Moths, are perhaps the most remarkable. *Metamimas australasiæ*, Don., *Cæquosa triangularis*, Don., *Chœrocampa erotus*, Cr., and the widely distributed *Protoparce convolvuli*, Linn., are abundant in the neighbourhood of Sydney. The family *Hepialidæ* contains some exceedingly fine species, including the beautiful *Charagiæ*, a group of moths which pass their larval condition, and undergo their transformations in cylindrical burrows which they make in the stems or branches of trees. Closely allied to the *Charagiæ* is the magnificent Giant Swift-moth, or "bent-wing," *Zelotypia Stacyi*, Sc., which is found in the Hunter River district. Female specimens of this moth sometimes measure as much as 10 inches across the wings. Those who wish to know more of these remarkable lignivorous moths should consult the late Mr. Scott's valuable paper on the subject, in the 2nd vol. of the N. S. Wales Entomological Society's Transactions, and Mr. Olliff's account of the habits of the larva, published in the Proceedings of the Linnean Society of N. S. Wales for 1887. The other great divisions of moths—the *Bombycina* (including the Silk-moths), the *Noctuina* (Night-moths), and the *Geometrina* (Loopers) are well represented.

The *Micro-Lepidoptera* abound. The *Oecophoridæ* alone, a family which is wonderfully prolific in Australia, are estimated at more than 2,000 species, of which a considerable number are found in and about Sydney. One of the largest and most beautiful genera of the Micros is *Cryptophasa*, a group containing conspicuous species, of which several are found near Sydney. The larvæ live in burrows in the stems of young *Banksiæ* and various shrubs, from which they emerge at night for the purpose of feeding on the leaves of the plant.

Diptera, or true Flies, have only a single pair of fully developed wings, the hinder pair existing as minute rudimentary organs, called "halteres," or "poisers." The thorax is highly developed and is usually more or less globular. The transformations are complete. The mosquitoes, or true gnats, belong to this group, and are only too well-known on account of the blood-sucking habits of the females, for, strange to say, it is this sex alone which feeds upon the blood of animals, and produces the humming or trumpeting noise, which so often disturbs us at night. The *Tipulidæ*, or Crane-flies, the *Mycetophilidæ*, or Fungus-gnats, the *Cecidomyidæ*, or Gall-gnats, the *Tabanidæ*, or Breeze-flies, the *Bombyliidæ*, or Humble-bee flies, and the *Muscidæ* (including the common House-fly and Blow-fly), are the most important families of this order. Certain species of the parasitic family *Hippoboscidæ* are found on our domestic animals, and are often very troublesome. The so-called sheep-tick, *Melophagus ovinus* (not to be confounded with the true ticks with eight legs, which belong to the Arachnida, an entirely different class), is a familiar example ; it is very flat, has no wings, and has the body much widened behind.

Aphaniptera include those insects, which in warm countries are at times only too familiar, the Fleas ; these creatures feed upon the blood of warm-blooded animals, and, in most cases each species of flea attaches itself to some particular animal. In Australia we have some very curious species, notably two, which are found on the Porcupine Ant-eater *(Echidna hystrix)*, one a gigantic species, *P. echidnæ*, Den., and the other a very remarkable form, *Echidnophaga ambulans*, Oll., which appears to have lost the power of jumping.

Rhynchota, or **Hemiptera** (Plant-bugs, Water-bugs, &c.), have a mouth formed for sucking, a large prothorax, and irregularly veined wings ; the fore-wings are often partly opaque and coriaceous. The transformations are incomplete. The order was divided by LATREILLE into two groups, the *Heteroptera*, or true bugs, and the *Homoptera*, the first containing a vast number of species, many of them most brilliantly coloured. The *Hydrocorisa*, a group containing many species, are aquatic in their habits. They are familiarly known as "water-scorpions" and "boatmen". A gigantic species of this group, the *Belostoma indicum*, St. F. & S., is sometimes very abundant. The *Hydrometridæ* are found upon the surface of pools and fresh water streams. The genus *Halobates* is marine, being found on the surface of the ocean, frequently at great distances from land. The *Homoptera* comprise insects of very diverse forms. The *Cicadidæ* (in Australia erroneously called locusts), hoppers, cuckoo-spit insects, the *Aphides*, and the *Coccididæ*, or scale-insects, are all well-known types belonging to this order. They all live on the juices of plants, some of them causing very considerable injuries, as in the case of the much dreaded vine pest, *Phylloxera vastatrix*, Pl., an insect belonging to the family *Aphididæ*.* Besides a large number of Coccididæ of the ordinary form, many of which are only too well known to fruit-growers and gardeners, we have a curious group of gall-making species (*Brachyscelinæ*) which are found, sometimes in great abundance, on various *Eucalypti*.

Orthoptera (Grasshoppers, Locusts, Crickets, Cockroaches, &c.) have the mouth-parts free and formed for biting. The fore-wings usually protect the hind-wings, which are net-veined. The transformations are incomplete. This order contains the *Gryllidæ*, or crickets, which are well represented; of this group we have a gigantic species, *Anatostoma australasiæ*, in which the jaws of the males are enormously developed. The *Acridiidæ*, or true locusts, are numerous; the well-known migratory species, *Oedipoda migratoria*, is occasionally found. The *Mantididæ*, the *Phasmidæ*, or walking-stick insects, and the *Blattidæ*, or cockroaches, all conspicuous types, are largely represented. The species of the tribe *Euplexoptera*, or earwigs, are also fairly numerous.

Thysanura include those destructive insects the *Lepismæ*, or "Silver-fish," and a great number of obscure forms.

---

* On a side-table is a case containing a series of preparations of *Phylloxera*, illustrating the life-history of the insect. Most of the specimens are mounted on slides for the microscope, and can only be examined by special application.

XII.

CRUSTACEA AND LOWER INVERTE-BRATA.

THE title adopted for this chapter is rather comprehensive; it is intended to include all the Invertebrata other than Mollusca and Insects, viz:—Part of the Arthropoda, the Vermes (or Worms), the Echinodermata, the Cœlenterata, and the Protozoa. The detailed classification of these will be found on page 19. A short description can only be given here. The specimens on view are in the room at north-end of upper floor.

Sub-Kingdom II.—ARTHROPODA.

Class I.—INSECTA has already been considered—see Chapter XI.

Classes II and III.—MYRIAPODA and ARACHNIDA are passed over in the meantime. Specimens are to be seen in Case 17.

Class IV.—CRUSTACEA.—The members of this class chiefly inhabit water; they breathe for the most part by gills; the body is divided into head, thorax, and abdomen; as a rule the head is fused with one or more of the thoracic segments, forming the cephalothorax. The head carries two pairs of antennæ, and the other appendages (legs, &c.) are carried by the thorax and abdomen. The Crustacea are divided into eight sub-classes; some of which, however, are too small for exhibition in the cases. It will, therefore, be unnecessary to describe such as are not represented in the collection.

Sub-class I.—ENTOMOSTRACA, is represented by the order Phyllopoda, whose species are mostly inhabitants of fresh water, and have bodies composed of many segments; they have leaf-like swimming feet, and a shield-like carapace, or in some representatives a laterally compressed bi-valve shell. *Lepidurus viridis* from Tasmania, and several species of the genus Apus from N. S. Wales, are examples. (See Case 17.)

Sub-class II.—XYPHOSURA or King Crabs, contains but two known species, both of which are represented in the collection, viz: *Limulus polyphemus* from North America, and *L. longispina* from the straits of Malacca. The body is covered by a large shield-like carapace, and the abdomen ends in a long spine-like tail. (See Case 17.)

Sub-class III.—EDRIOPHTHALMA, or sessile-eyed Crustacea, contains two orders :— (See Case 12.)

1. **Amphipoda**, in which the branchiæ consist of membranous vesicles at the bases of the legs. The thorax has six or seven free segments, and the abdomen seven segments, the terminal segment being adapted for swimming. Examples — *Orchestia macleayana*, and *Leucothoë novæ-hollandiæ*.

2. **Isopoda.**—In this order the body is broad and depressed; the head is distinct from the thorax; the latter consists of seven free segments, each bearing a pair of legs, all, except the first pair being alike; the branchial lamellæ are placed under the abdomen. Examples—*Idotea excavata, Porcellio obtusifrons, Sphæroma lævis*, and *Cymodocea pubescens*.

Sub-class IV. — PODOPHTHALMA or stalk-eyed Crustacea, includes the shrimps, lobsters, crayfishes, and crabs. These are characterised by having their eyes on movable stalks, and by the head being more or less fused with the thoracic segments, forming the carapace which covers and protects the body. In the order **Stomatopoda** the branchiæ are external, and are usually attached to the under surface of the abdomen; the latter is elongate, and ends in a powerful tail, which is the chief organ of locomotion. Examples—*Lysiosquilla brazieri, Squilla miles*, and *Gonodactylus chiragra.* (See Case 12.)

Sub-class V.—DECAPODA, or ten-footed Crustacea, has the branchiæ enclosed in a special cavity on each side of the body ; and five pairs of legs, the first of which terminates in two-fingered claws.   The sub-class is divided into three orders :—

1. **Brachyura** (short-tailed).—The abdomen is short and reduced to a triangular or rounded tail without caudal fin, and is sunk into an excavation on the ventral surface of the thorax.   *Stenorhynchus fissifrons, Hyastenus diacanthus, Paramithrax sternocostulatus, Parthenope horrida, Ateragatis floridus, Thalamita crucifera, Gelasimus vocans, Talitrus sylvatics, Grapsus variegatus, Calappa hepatica,* and *Leucosia splendida,* are examples of the principal families.   (See Cases 13 and 14).

2. **Anomura** (irregular-tailed). — The abdomen is but slightly developed, except in the *Paguridæ.   Dromia excavata, Lomis hirta, Remipes testudinaria, Ranina dentata, Eupagurus sinuatus* and the great land crab *Birgus latro* are examples.   (See Cases 11 and 13).

3. **Macrura** (long-tailed).—The abdomen is strongly developed, provided with four or five pairs of abdominal feet, and terminating in a well-developed five-parted tail.   Examples: *Galathea australiensis, Ibacus peronii, Palinurus hugelii, Astacopsis serratus, Alpheus edwardsii,* and *Penœus canaliculatus.*   (See Case 12).

Sub-Kingdom III.—VERMES, or WORMS.

The classes into which this sub-kingdom is divided are widely different from each other, and within our limits little information can be given about them.   The body is generally soft, elongate or vermiform, bilaterally symmetrical, with or without feet, which, when present, are never jointed.   Specimens of the most important will be shortly exhibited.

Class I.—The PLATYHELMINTHES are more or less flattened worms of a very simple organisation, and without any true segments.   There are three orders in this class :—

1.—**Turbellaria,** which possess a digestive cavity, have the skin covered with cilia, and are non-parasitic. This order includes the *Planarian* and *Nemertean* worms, the former of which exist in the sea, in fresh water, and in damp forest lands. (See Case 17.)

2.—**Trematoda,** which are usually internal parasitic worms, provided with one, two, or more ventral suckers. The species of this order are numerous ; they are found on the gills of fishes, on crustacea, and in the blood vessels and intestines of various animals. The Liver-fluke of sheep, *Distoma hepatica,* is perhaps the best known example. (See Case 17.)

3.—**Cestoda,** which are internal parasites usually of an elongate and flattened form ; the head is provided with hooks, spines, or suckers ; the digestive cavity is absent. The Tapeworm, *Tænia solium* is a familiar representative of the order. (See Case 17.)

Class II.—The NEMATHELMINTHES or Threadworms are mostly internal parasites, many of them too small to be exhibited, except with the aid of a microscope. The "vinegar" and "paste" eels *Anguillulæ,* the Guineaworm *Filaria medinensis,* and the *Trichina spiralis,* found as a parasite in man and causing the disease trichinosis, are examples.

Class III.—The GEPHYREA.—This is a small class formerly associated with the Echinoderms. It comprises marine worms with a cylindrical body, a thick coriaceous skin, unsegmented, but often indistinctly ringed, mouth with or without tentacles, and head, not distinct from the body, often produced into a long proboscis. The following genera are represented in the collection : *Sipunculus, Phascolosoma, Bonellia, Phymosoma,* and *Phoronis.* (See Case 17.)

Class IV.—The ANNELIDA.—In this class there are four orders :— (See Case 17.)

1. **Hirudinea,** including the leeches, and composed mostly of aquatic animals provided with a sucking disc at one or both ends of the body. The *Hirudo quinquestriata,* or Medicinal Leech, is an example of this order.

2. **Oligochæta.**—In this order are included the Earth-worms, which, in some parts of Australia, attain gigantic proportions. *Megascolides australis* occurs in Gippsland, and when extended is sometimes six feet in length ; in New South Wales are found *Notoscolex grandis*, and *N. camdenensis*, the latter from eighteen inches to two feet, and the former from two feet six inches to three feet six inches in length.

3. **Chætopoda.** — Marine worms usually provided with tubular setigerous feet termed "parapodia" ; external branchiæ on the dorsal surface, which, however, are often absent or rudimentary ; head in most cases distinct and provided with tentacles. Examples—*Aphrodite australis*, or Sea Mouse, *Lepidonotus melanogrammus, Syllis corruscans*, and *Nereilepas amblyodonta*.

4. **Cepholobranchia.**—In this order the branchiæ are on or near the head. The body has the regions well defined and is protected by a tube, which is either membranous, calcareous, or composed of sand grains cemented together. *Serpula vasifera, Sabella velata, Vermilia cœspitosa*, and *Spirographis australiensis*, are examples from Sydney Harbour.

Class V.—The POLYZOA.—This class consists of minute marine animals forming colonies which either assume an erect plant-like aspect or spread over stones, shells, &c., and are composed of vast numbers of cells, in which the polypides reside ; the mouth is surrounded by a circle of ciliated tentacles. There are three sub-orders in this class :—(See Case 1.)

1. **Chilostomata,** is characterised by having the cell opening or mouth closed by a movable lip or operculum. Examples—*Catenicella ventricosa, Bugula neritina, Flustra dissimilis, Adeona cellulosa*, and *Selenaria maculata*.

2. **Cyclostomata,** has the mouth or cell aperture round, and without a movable operculum. *Idmonia milneana* and *Mesentipora repens* are examples.

3. **Ctenostomata,** has the cell aperture closed by a series of marginal seta. *Amathia bicornis*.

Sub-Kingdom IV.—ECHINODERMATA.

The Echinodermata consist of marine animals with a radiate arrangement, having usually five rays or arms, but often more; the skin is charged with calcareous bodies in the form of spicules or plates, occuring either as separate masses, or variously combined so as to form a continuous skeleton, as in the sea-eggs.

The Echinodermata are divided into five sub-classes.

Sub-Class I.—The **CRINOIDEA** or Feather Stars.—This sub-class is represented in the collection by *Pentacrinus caput-medusae*, *Antedon pumila*, *Actinometra solaris*, &c. The first named is a stalked form which is attached to rocks on the sea bottom throughout its life, whilst the two latter are stalked only for a short time in their young state, the adult animal being free-swimming. (See Case 2.)

Sub-Class II.—The **ASTEROIDEA** or Star Fishes, which are chiefly characterised by the five-rayed star-like shape of the body, the ambulacral feet being confined to the ventral surface of the body, and the skeletal plates of the ambulacral area being articulated together like vertebrae. There are four orders in this sub-class :—

1. **Asteriadæ**, with four rows of ambulacral tube feet, each terminating in an expanded disc, which acts like the sucking discs of the Octopus. Examples—*Asterias calamaria*, *A. polyplax*, *Uniophora globifera*, *Stichaster australis*, *Heliaster helianthus*, *H. microbrachia*, and *H. kubingii*. (See Case 5.)

2. **Solasteridæ**, with the ambulacral feet in two rows. Examples—*Solaster decanus*, *Echinaster purpureus*, *Linckia pacifica*, *Anthenea acuta*, *Pentaceros nodosus*, *Pentagonaster dubenii*, *Asterina calcar*, *A. exigua*, and *A. gunnii*. (See Cases 3, 4, and 5.)

3. **Astropectinidæ**.—In this order the ambulacral feet are conical and devoid of the disc-like terminal suckers. Examples—*Astropecten polyacanthus*, *A. triseriatus*, *Luidia maculata*, and *Archaster typicus*. (See Cases 2 and 3.)

Sub-Class III.—The **OPHIUROIDEA**, or Sand or Brittle Stars.—The members of this sub-class are characterised by their disc-shaped body, long rounded arms, and by the ambulacral grooves being covered in by a series of calcareous plates, or by soft skin. There are two orders :—

1. **Ophiuridæ**, in which the arms are simple. Examples— *Ophiopeza conjungens, Pectinura marmorata, Ophiolepis annulosa, Ophionereis schayeri, Ophiocoma brevipes,* and *Ophiothrix longipeda.* (See Case 2.)

2. **Euryalidæ**, which have the arms branched and the ambulacral groove covered by soft skin. Examples— *Euryale aspera* and *Gorgonocephalus australis.* (See Case 2.)

Sub-Class IV.—The **ECHINOIDEA**, or Sea Urchins.—In this sub-class the body is enclosed in a more or less conical shell or test, formed of numerous calcareous plates. These plates are provided with spines, and are arranged in five ambulacral and five inter-ambulacral double rows. The ambulacral plates are perforated to allow of the protrusion of the tube feet, whilst the inter-ambulacral plates carry the spines. The Echinoidea are divided into three orders :— (See Cases 6 and 7.)

1. **Cidaridea.**—The animals composing which are usually regular, having the anal aperture in the apical region, with the ambulacral areas equal and band like. Examples— *Cidaris metularia, Phyllacanthus australis, Goniocidaris tubaria, Centrostephanus rodgersii, Heterocentrotus mammillatus, Strongylocentrotus erythrogrammus, Salmacis alexandri, Amblypneustes ovum,* and *Tripneustes angulosus.*

2. **Clypeastridea,** which have an irregular depressed body, the mouth being central and furnished with teeth, and the anus eccentric. The ambulacral areas radiate from the apex and are rosette-shaped. Examples : *Fibularia australis, Laganum peronii, Arachnoides placenta,* and *Echinodiscus auritus.*

3. **Spatangidea.**—In this order the body is more or less irregularly heart-shaped, both mouth and posterior opening on the lower side eccentric, the teeth absent, and the ambulacral areas petaloid, often only four-leaved. *Echinoneus cyclostomus*, *Maretia planulata*, *Breynia australasiæ*, *Echinocardium australe*, *Hemiaster apicatus*, and *Schizaster ventricosus* are good examples.

Sub-Class V.—The **HOLOTHUROIDEA**, or Sea Cucumbers, Bech-de-mer, Trepang, &c.—In this sub-class the body is elongated, with a thick leather-like skin, which contains numerous calcareous spicules resembling wheels, anchors, latticed plates, hooks, &c.; the mouth is surrounded by a series of contractile tentacles, which are often branched and plume-like. There are two orders in this sub-class :—   (See Case 17.)

1. **Pedata**, with usually five rows of ambulacral feet. Examples—*Holothuria vagabunda*, *Colochirus australis*, *Thyone okeni*, *Thyone spinosus*, and *Phyllophorus perspicillum*.

2. **Apoda**, without ambulacral feet. Examples—*Chirodota japonica*, *C. australina*, and *Synapta dolobrifera*.

Sub-Kingdom V.—COELENTERATA.

In this group are included the Sponges, Jelly-fishes, Sea-Anemones, Corals, and Hydroid Zoophytes. These all possess a central body cavity, which serves alike for circulation and digestion; they are radially symmetrical, and are composed of many cells. There are three divisions of this sub-kingdom—the Hydrozoa, or Jelly-fishes and Zoophytes; the Actinozoa, or Corals; and the Porifera or Sponges.*

Division I.—HYDROZOA.

Contains Polyps with a simple gastric cavity in which the mesenteric lamellæ are altogether absent, or only exist in a very rudimentary condition. The sexual generation assumes the form either of free-swimming Medusæ, or of rudimentary medusoid buds, which are not separated from the parent body. Colonies of Hydrozoa usually consist of tree-like stocks.

---

* See Lendenfeld's Catalogue of Sponges, No. 13 Museum series.

The first two classes of this division are represented in the collection, the *Scyphomedusæ* or Jelly-fishes by *Phyllorhiza punctata* (type specimen); and the *Siphonophora* by *Physalia megalista* (the Portuguese man-of-war), and by specimens of *Porpita, Velella, and Diphyes*, the only Australian genera. (See Case 17.)

Class III. — The HYDROMEDUSÆ. — This class is largely represented in the collection. It is divided into three orders :—

1.—**Hydrocorralliæ.**—Coral-like polyps with stocks having a calcareous skeleton, tubular hydrothecæ, and two kinds of polyps, some possessing a stomatic cavity, which in others is wanting. *Millepora alcicornis, Stylaster gracilis,* and *Distichopora violacea* are well known species. (See Case 10.)

2.—**Tubulariæ.**—Polyps without hydrothecæ, the stems only in some cases having a chitinous envelope. *Tubularia gracilis* and *Pennaria australis* are examples. (See Case 17.)

3.—**Campanulariæ.**—The members of this order usually present many branched plant-like tufts, possessing cup-shaped hydrothecæ, into which, in most cases, the polyp heads can retire at will. The following are the chief families into which it is divided :—

Family I. *Plumulariidæ.*—In the animals composing this family the hydrothecæ are arranged in single rows, usually on the upper surfaces of the branches, and have small accessory cups containing stinging cells or nematocysts. *Plumularia rubra Aglaophenia divaricata,* and *Halicornaria ascidioides,* all from Port Jackson, are representatives of the family. (See Case 17.)

Family II. *Sertulariidæ.*—Often much branched, with flask-shaped hydrothecæ arranged in opposite or alternating rows on each side of the stems and branches. *Sertularia elongata, Diphasia pinnata, Sertularella divaricata, Pasythea quadridentata, Idia pristis,* and *Thuiara lata* are good examples of the family. See Case 17.)

Family III. *Campanulariidæ.* — Either simple or branched, the hydrothecæ forming terminal cups to the branches. Species of this and the preceding family are obtainable both in Port Jackson and on seaweeds at some of the outer beaches, *Idia pristis* excepted. Specimens exhibited are *Campanularia tincta, Obelia geniculata, Eucopella campanularia, Lineolaria spinulosa,* and *Lafoea scandens.* (See Case 17.)

Division II —ACTINOZOA.

Class IV.—ZOANTHARIA.—In this class we have the Sea Anemones, and the true corals. These have the mouth surrounded by a series of tentacles numbering either six or some multiple of six : they possess a tubular digestive cavity separated from the body walls by the perivisceral space, which is subdivided into a number of compartments by a series of vertical lamellæ, or folds. They are separated into three orders :—

1.—**Actinidæ**, the members of which are the well known Sea Anemones, and are characterised by having the power of motion, by being rarely compound, and by an absence of hard parts, or corallum : the family is represented by a series of glass models, and a number of specimens from the Zoological Station of Naples, exhibited in Cases 1 and 16.

2.—**Antipathidæ.**—These are simple or branched polyp stocks with an internal horny skeleton, and, having the mouth surrounded by six tentacles. A fine example from North Australia, *Antipathes cupressus,* may be seen in Case 15.

3.—**Madreporaria.**—Corals with a continuous calcareous skeleton, classified in two sections.

Section (A) Aporosa.—In this section are included—

1. The *Turbinolidæ,* which mostly consist of single corals with a well-developed calcareous corallum, having very distinct septa and an imperforate covering or theca. Examples— *Flabellum* sp., *Caryophyllia smithii.* (See Case 9.)

2. The *Oculinidœ*, which are usually hard branched corals, with but few septa developed in cups of the corallum. *Oculina diffusa* and *Amphihelia infundibulifera* are representatives of this family. (See Cases 9 and 10.)

3. The *Astrœidœ*, or Star Corals, which are usually of large size, and form either rounded masses as in the brain coral, or tufted clusters of simple stems. The septa are mostly produced into sharp denticulata or cutting edges. *Astrœa denticulata*, *Eusmilia knorri*, *Galaxea esperi*, *Cœlora labyrinthiformis* are examples of this family. (See Case 9.)

4. The *Fungiidœ*, or Mushroom Corals.—These usually consist of large flat single cups with many strongly developed septa. The following are representatives of this family— *Fungia danai*, *F. repanda*, and *F. patella*. (See Cases 9 and 10.)

Section (B) Perforata.—This section includes only one family—

The *Madreporidœ*.—Most of the members of this family are large branching species with small cups, and the septa little developed. *Madrepora echinata*, *Dendrophyllia nigrescens*, and *D. ramea* are examples. (See Case 10).

Class V.—ALCYONARIA.—This order includes the following families : *Alcyonidœ*, or soft corals; *Pennatulidœ*, or sea-pens; *Gorgoniidœ*; and *Tubiporidœ*. They possess eight plumed tentacles, and the same number of vertical lamellœ, or mesenteries.

1. The Alcyonidæ are usually called soft corals, on account of the absence of a continuous hard skeleton : they form lobed or finger-like clusters studded with polyps, having a kind of leathery consistence and the epidermis usually charged with calcareous spicules. Examples are *Spongodes florida*, *Nephthya chabrolii* and *Alcyonium* sp. from Port Jackson, *Alcyonium palmatum*, from Naples, preserved with the polyps extended. (See Case 17.)

2. The Pennatulidæ or Sea-pens, are feather-like polyps, having a horny or calcareous axis; the polyps are confined to the upper part of the stem, and are arranged on leaf-like pinnules, either irregularly around a cylindrical head on one side of a

H

kidney-shaped lobe, or disposed in a terminal cluster. Examples—
Pennatula rubra, *P. phosphorea*, *Sarcophyllum grande*, *Clavella
australasiæ*, *Renilla reniformis*, and *Osteocella verrillii*, the last
being about six feet in length. (See Case 17.)

3. The **Gorgoniidæ** are mostly large branched polyps with
a horny or calcareous axis surrounded by a thin layer of flesh, in
in which the polyps are imbedded; the whole of the fleshy substance
is often charged with spicules. *Rhipidogorgia flabellum*, *Xiphogor-
gia anceps*, *Verrucella gemmacea*, *Mopsella coccinea*, *Melithæa
ochracea*, *Primnoa australasiæ*, *Isis*, sp., and *Corallum rubrum*,
the last being the well-known red coral of commerce, may be
mentioned as examples. (See Case 15.)

4. The **Tubiporidæ** or Organ Corals, usually form large masses
of a bright red colour, consisting of a vast number of calcareous
tubes connected by horizontal plates. Example — *Tubipora
musica*. (See Case 15.)

Division III.—PORIFERA.

Class VI.—PORIFERA or Sponges.—In this division the
body has a spongy consistence, and is strengthened by a calcareous,
siliceous, or horny skeleton. There is a series of inhalent pores
passing from the outside to the inner ciliated passages, and one
or more exhalent apertures. The water passes in by means of
the former, and out by the latter, the movement being caused by
the action of the flagellate cells lining the body cavity.

The Collections, which include very many of the types collected
by the Museum staff in Port Jackson and described by Dr. R.
von Lendenfeld, are to be seen in Cases 18 and 19.

The **Myxospongia** are represented by *Bajalus lacus*, which
is a soft gelatinous sponge without hard parts or skeleton.

The **Calcispongia** are represented, among others, by
Sycandra arborea, and *S. ramsayi* ; the former exhibits tree-like
clusters with cylindrical branches and a smooth surface, the latter
rounded sac-like bodies clothed with long calcareous spicules.

The **Siliceous Sponges** are represented by the *Euplectella
aspergillum*, or Venus's Flower basket; and by *Hyalonema
sieboldii*, or Glass Rope Sponge from Japan, which has the upper

part of the spicules covered by a species of Polythoa, an Alcyon-arian coral, which lives as a commensal with the sponge. Another important and rare species from the "Porcupine" expedition is the *Hollenia Carpenteri*.

The Ceratospongia, or Horny Sponges, to which the common "Toilet Sponge" belongs, are largely represented. Amongst those on exhibit are some varieties of the commercial sponge found on the Australian coast.

Sub-Kingdom VI.—PROTOZOA.

This sub-kingdom consists of animals of small size, extremely simple, and destitute of any definite cell-tissues. It includes all the lower forms of animal life, such as Infusoria, Gregarina, Amœba, Radiolaria, and Foraminifera.

The Foraminifera is the only group at present represented in the Collection. The bodies of animals in this group consist of jelly-like masses, or sarcode. They are capable of throwing out from the mouth, or through perforations scattered over the surface of the shell or test, long foot-like processes, called pseudopoda or "false feet." The shells of these animals are usually composed of carbonate of lime or of sand grains cemented together, and they may be either single or many chambered. This sub-kingdom is represented in the cases by a series of specimens from Port Jackson as well as by a set of greatly enlarged models. Some of the specimens may be compared with the models, as for instance *Peneroplis planatus*, which will give some idea of the relative size of the species. (See Case 1.)

XIII.

OSTEOLOGY OR SKELETONS.

OSTEOLOGY is the Science which treats of the Bones. The Skeletons in the Museum are in two rooms at the south end of the ground floor, called the Osteological Halls, and are arranged as nearly as possible in accordance with the classification of Vertebrates, as at present accepted, beginning on the left hand side with the Human Skeletons. The animals, to which the skeletons belong, are referred to in the chapters on Mammals, Birds, Fishes, Reptiles, &c., and need not be again noticed, but a short description of a human skeleton is given, as MAN is the highest type of a vertebrate animal, and it is desirable to have a knowledge of the bones composing his skeleton in order properly to understand the others.

The following is a list of the bones in the Human Skeleton :—

Vertebræ or Back-bones — Cervical or Neck Vertebræ, 7; Dorsal or Back Vertebræ, 12; Lumbar or Loin Vertebræ, 5 ; Sacral, and Coccygeal or Caudal Vertebræ formed in youth of 5 in the Sacrum, and 4 in the Coccyx anchylosed in maturity, 2 ; making in all.......................... 26

Bones of the Head—8 in the Cranium and 14 in the Face, considered as one piece, and the Lower Jaw as another 2

Tongue or Hyoid Bone, shaped something like the letter U.............. 1

Ribs—12 on each side.................... 24

Breast Bones (*Sternum*)—2 large and 1 small, which become anchylosed with age 1

Collar Bones (*Clavicles*)-1 on each side   2

Shoulder Blades (*Scapulæ*)—1 on each
side   2

Arm Bones (*Humerus, Ulna, Radius*)—
3 in each arm...........................   6

Hand—Wrist or Carpal Bones, 8;
Metacarpal Bones, 5; Thumb, 3;
Fingers, 4, with 3 Bones each = 12;
making 27 in each hand............   54

Pelvis or Hip Bones—1 on each side
(in the young in 3 pieces, anchylosed
with age)......................   2

Leg Bones (*Femur, Tibia, Fibula,
Patella* or knee cap)—4 in each leg   8

Foot—Ankle, 7; Metatarsus, 5; Great
Toe, 2; other Toes, 4, with 3 Bones
each = 12; making 26 in each foot...   52
                                         ——

Total separate Bones............ 180

The characteristic Bone is the Back Bone. It is composed of
a number of separate bones called Vertebræ, which are shaped
something like rings, and are placed one against another with an
elastic tissue uniting them.   They are hard and massive in
front, but thin behind, with sharp processes or points projecting
and forming a line down the back—hence the name spine.
Together they form a long tube which, in the living animal,
contains the spinal marrow.   It is from this that the sub-kingdom
Vertebrata takes its name.

The Skull consists of 22 bones, which in infancy are separate,
but in youth become dovetailed together and united so firmly
as to practically form one piece.   In one of the Cases is exhibited a disarticulated skull showing the shape and position of
these separate bones.   The interior of the skull is occupied by
the Brain, and is called the "Brain Cavity." The Cranium or
Skull consists properly of 8 bones, but there are 14 Bones of the
Face attached to it and usually spoken of as forming part of it.
The Lower Jaw is attached by a joint, but does not form part of

it. There are 32 Teeth, viz.—In front, the Incisors or Cutting Teeth, of which there are 4 in each jaw; next to these, the Canines or Eye Teeth, 1 on each side in both upper and lower jaws; then the Bicuspids, so called from having projections or cusps on the surface, of which there are 3 on each side of each jaw; and last, the Back Teeth, Molars, or Grinding Teeth, of which also there are 3 on each side of each jaw. The number and position of the teeth are usually expressed by the following formula :—Incisors, $\frac{2 \cdot 2}{2 \cdot 2} = 8$; Canines, $\frac{1 \cdot 1}{1 \cdot 1} = 4$; Bicuspids, $\frac{2 \cdot 2}{2 \cdot 2} = 8$; Molars, $\frac{3 \cdot 3}{3 \cdot 3} = 12$. Total, $\frac{16}{16}$ or 32. The teeth, however, are not considered part of the skeleton.

The Ribs are long curved narrow bones—12 on each side. They are attached behind to the back-bone and in front to the breast-bone by bands of cartilage or gristle. They form the sides of a kind of box called the " Chest," in which the heart and lungs are placed.

The Collar-Bones are narrow curved bones extending from the top of the Breast-bone to the shoulders.

The Shoulder Blades are flat and somewhat triangular shaped bones and form the back parts of the shoulders. The sockets in which the arms move are at the upper corners of these bones.

The Arm Bones are :—In the upper arm, one bone called the *humerus*; in the fore arm, two bones, the *ulna* and the *radius*.

The Wrist is composed of 8 small bones placed between the two bones of the fore arm and the bones of the hand.

The Hand has five long narrow bones; one leads to the Thumb, the others lead each to a finger. The Fingers have each 3 bones, but the Thumb has only 2.

The Pelvis or Hip Bones are large massive flattened bones, one on each side. They receive the lower end of the back-bone and connect the vertebræ with the legs. They have consequently to carry the entire weight of the body and any load it may bear.

The Leg Bones are :—The Thigh or *femur*, a large strong bone forming the upper part of the leg; the two bones of the leg, the larger called the Shin or *tibia*, and the smaller called the Splint-bone or *fibula*; and the Knee-cap or *patella*.

The Ankle is formed of a series of 7 little bones between the leg and the foot. One of them works in the lower end of the bones of the leg and forms the ankle joint, while another projects to form the heel, and is called the *os calsis*.

The Foot has five bones as in the hand, but they are curved to form the instep. The Toes have bones similar to the fingers in number, but modified in shape to suit the different uses to which they are put. The foot is supported on three points, the heel, the ball of the great toe, and the ball of the little toe. The arch is sustained by a strong ligament which stretches from the heel to the toes.

The Skeleton in the living animal is covered with about 400 muscles, which are attached by sinews to the bones. Motion is obtained by the contracting and thickening of these muscles and is imparted to the bones through the sinews. The ends of the bones at the joints are covered with a fine smooth layer of gristle, and they are attached to each other by strong ligaments. Most of the bones are hollow, and many contain a fatty substance called marrow; they are covered in life with a thin skin well supplied with blood vessels, and the joints are kept soft by a fluid resembling oil.

Such is the human Skeleton. In the lower vertebrata various modifications are found. In Quadrupeds the arms become legs, in Birds they become wings, in Fishes both arms and legs are represented by fins; in some animals the vertebræ are greatly increased in number by the addition of a tail, and there are many other differences which an inspection of the specimens in the Cases will show. The following short table has been prepared to assist in comparing the number of vertebræ in some of the higher animals :—

VERTEBRÆ.	Man.	Gorilla.	Bear.	Lion.	Dog.	Horse.	Cow.	Baleen Whale.	Three-toed Sloth.	Manatee.	Perch.	Blue Pointer Shark.	Mullet.	Eel.	Ostrich.	Pythons.
Cervical......	7	7	7	7	7	7	7	7	9	6	...	...	...	...	17	...
Dorsal	12	13	15	13	13	19	13	15	15 or 17	15 to 18	...	...	...	...	8	...
Lumbar......	5	4	6	7	7	5	6	10	5 or 3		21	60	11	45	10	...
Sacral	5	5	5	3	3	5	5	...	6	25 to 29	...	...	...	...	3	...
Coccygeal ... or Caudal	4	0	8	23	22	17	21	27	11	‡	20*	125	13	71	18	...
Total ...	33	29	41	53	52	53	52	59	46	46 to 53	41	185	24	116	56	300†

* Sometimes 21. † And often considerably over that number. ‡ Has no sacral vertebræ.

LIST OF THE PRINCIPAL SKELETONS IN THE MUSEUM,

With reference to the Cases where they are exhibited.

Class I.—MAMMALIA.

ORDER I.—BIMANA OR HUMAN SKELETONS.

(Exhibited in Cases 1 and 2.)

Australian Aboriginals—Six specimens.
Dis-articulated Skull, showing shape and position of the several bones.
Collection of about 300 Human Skull, of various races and from different countries.

ORDER II.—QUADRUMANA OR MONKEYS.

(Exhibited in Cases 1 and 2.)

Gorilla, *Troglodytes gorilla.*
Chimpanzee, *Troglodytes niger.*
Orang-Outang, *Simia satyrus.*
Grey Baboon, *Cynocephalus hama-dryas.*
A Monkey's Skeleton (dis-articulated).

White-Throated Sapagon Monkey, *Cebus hypoleucus*
Skeletons of Monkeys (Various).
Pig-tailed Monkey, *Macacus neme-strinus.*
Aye-Aye, *Chiromys madagascariensis.*

ORDER III.—CARNIVORA.

(Exhibited in Cases 3, 4, 9 and 10.)

Lion, *Felis leo*
Lioness Cub, 8 months old
Bengal Tiger, *Felis tigris.*
Hyæna, *Hyæna striata.*
Domestic Cat, *Felis domestica.*
Dog, *Canis familiaris.*
Bull Dog
Kangaroo Dog
Dog, cross between Newfoundland and St. Bernard breeds.
Dingo or Native Dog, *Canis dingo.*

Wolf, *Canis lupus.*
American Wolf, *Canis occidentalis.*
Wolverene, *Gulo borealis.*
Bear, *Ursus ferox or americanus*
Polar Bear, *Thallarctus maritimus.*
Coati, *Nasua nasuta.*
Cotimundi, *Nasua sp.*
Sea Leopard, *Stenorhynchus leptonyx*
Seal, *Phoca vitulina*
Seal, *Arctocephalus cinereus*
Walrus (skull), *Trichecus rosmarus.*

ORDER IV.— INSECTIVORA.

(Exhibited in Case 4.)

Common Mole, *Talpa europœa.*

ORDER V.—CHIROPTERA.

(Exhibited in Case 4.)

Flying Fox, *Pteropus poliocephalus*

ORDER VI.—RODENTIA.

(Exhibited in Case 4.)

Mongoose, *Herpestes mungo.*
Do. *Herpestes paludosus.*
Ferret, *Putorius vulgaris.*

Racoon, *Procyon lotor.*
Guinea Pig, *Cavea aperea.*
Jerboa, *Dipus œgyptius.*

ORDER VII.—UNGULATA.

(Exhibited in Cases 5 and 6 and on the floor.)

Indian Elephant, *Elephas indicus.*
Cape Coney, *Hyrax capensis.*
Rhinoceros, *Rhinoceros sumatrensis.*
Horse, *Equus caballus.*
Burchell's Zebra, *Equus burchelli.*
Hippopotamus, *Hippopotamus amphibius.*
Wild Egyptian Goat, *Capra œgagra.*
Rocky Mountain Sheep, *Capriana montana.*
Giraffe, *Camelopardalis giraffa.*
Gazelle, *Gazella dorcus.*

Eland, *Oreas canna.*
Wild Pig, *Sus papuensis.*
Dromedary, *Camelus dromedarius*
Bactrian Camel, *Camelus bactrianus.*
Llama, *Llama paca.*
Goat, *Capra hercus.*
Great Irish Elk (now extinct), *Megaceros hibernicus.*
Fallow Deer, *Dama vulgaris.*
Chevrotain, *Tragulus napu.*
Musmon or Sardinian Wild Sheep, *Ovis musmon.*

ORDER VIII.—CETACEA.

(Exhibited in Cases 7, 8, 9, 10, and elsewhere as marked.)

Baleen Whale, *Balæna antipodarum.*
Do *Balæna novæ-hollandiæ.*
Do. *Balæna marginalis.*
Sperm Whale, *Physeter macrocephalus,* overhead in Australian Hall.
Hand of Sperm Whale.
Small Sperm Whale, *Mesoplodon thomsoni*—Above Case 13.
Do. (skull), *Mesoplodon layardi.*
Do., *Mesoplodon seychellensis* — Above Case 12.
Arm of long-armed Whale, *Megaptera longimana*—Above Cases.

Grey's Sperm Whale, *Kogia grayi.*
Skull of a Whale, *Ulodon grayi.*
Ziphioid Whale (skull), *Petrorhynchus, sp.*
Dolphin, *Delphinus, sp.*
Do. *Tursio catalania.*
Grampus, *Orca, sp.*
Skulls of various species of Dolphins, *Delphinus, sp.*
Freshwater Porpoise, *Plataanista gangetica.*

ORDER IX.—SIRENIA.

(Exhibited in Cases 9 and 10.)

Manatee, *Manatus americanus.*
Do. (skulls) ,,   ,,

Dugong, *Halicore dugong.*
Steller's Sea Cow, *Rhytina stelleri.*

ORDER X.—EDENTATA.

(Exhibited in Case 4.)

Sloth, *Bradypus tridactylus.*
Great Ant Eater, *Myrmecophaga jubata.*

Two - fingered Sloth, *Cholœpus didactylus.*

ORDER XI.—MARSUPIALIA.

(Exhibited in Case 2.)

Kangaroo, *Macropus major.*
Black Wallaroo, *Osphranter robustus.*
Wallaby, *Halmaturus rufficollis.*
Brush Wallaby, *Halmaturus ualabatus.*
Tasmanian Wallaby, *Halmaturus billardieri.*
Black-striped Wallaby, *Halmaturus dorsalis.*
Pademelon Wallaby, *Halmaturus thetidis.*
Skull of Hypsiprymnodon.

Long-nosed Bandicoot, *Perameles nasuta.*
Native Cat, *Dasyurus viverrinus.*
Tiger Cat, *Dasyurus maculatus.*
Tasmanian Devil, *Sarcophilus ursinus.*
Tasmanian Tiger, *Thylacinus cynocephalus.*
Wombat, *Phascolomys wombat.*
Do.   *Phascolomys latifrons.*
Do.   *Phascolomys lasiorhinus.*
Native Bear, *Phascolarctus cinereus.*

ORDER XII.—MONOTEMATA.

(Exhibited in Case 2.)

Echidna, *Echidna aculeata*

Platypus, *Ornithorynchus anatinus.*

Class II.—AVES or BIRDS.

(Exhibited in Cases 8, 18, and 19.)

In CASE 8—

Ostrich, *Struthio camelus.*
Emu, *Dromæus novæ-hollandiæ.*
Moa, *Dinornis crassus.*
Great Horned Owl. *Bubo maximus.*
Secretary Bird, *Serpentarius secretarius.*

Moruck, *Casuarius bennetti.*
Jabiru, *Xenorhynchus australis,* var.
Pelican, *Pelecanus conspicillatus.*
White-tailed Eagle, *Haliaëtus albicilla*

In CASE 18—

New Holland Darter, *Plotus novæhollandiæ.*
Australian Grebe, *Podiceps australis.*
Peacock, *Pavo cristatus.*

Toucan or Hornbill, *Buceros plicatus*
Black Swan, *Cygnus atratus.*
Bustard, *Eupodotis australis.*

In Case 19.

Cockatoo, *Cacatua ophthalmica.*
White Cockatoo, *Cacatua galerita,* aged 100 years.
Broad-tailed Parrot, *Platycercus per-sonatus.*
Lyre Bird, *Menura superba.*
Common Magpie,*Gymnorhina tibicen.*
Satin Bower Bird, *Ptilonorhynchus holosericeus.*
Crested Pigeon, *Goura coronata.*
Peaceful Dove, *Geopelia placida.*
Cape Barron Goose, *Cereopsis novæ-hollandiæ.*
Wandering Albertros, *Diomedia exulans.*
Black Eye-browed do., *Diomedia melanophrys.*

Kiwi, *Apteryx australis.*
Owen's Kiwi, *Apteryx oweni.*
Pelican, *Pelecanus onocrotalus.*
Curlew, *Numenius uropygialis.*
Great Sea Eagle, *Haliaëtus leucogaster.*
Many Coloured Eclectus,*Electus polychloris.*
Stone Plover, *Ædicnemus grallarius.*
Kakapo, *Stringops habroptilus.*
Nightingale, *Lusciola philomela.*
Humming Bird.
Giant Petrel, *Ossifraga gigantea.*
Kingfisher, *Alcedo ispida.*
Water Hen, *Gallinula tribonyx.*
Tree Pipit, *Anthus arboreus.*
Musk Duck, *Biziura lobata.*

Class III.—REPTILIA.

(In Case 8, or as marked).

Turtle, *Chelymys macquaria*
Green Turtle, *Chelonia mydas*
Lace Lizard, *Hydrosaurus varius*
Sleeping Lizard, *Cyclodus nigroluteus*
Diamond Snake, *Morelia spilotes*
Black Snake,*Pseudechis porphyriacus*
Chameleon, *Chameleon africanus*
Crocodile, *Crocodilus bipocatus*
  In Case 12
Crocodile, *Crocodilus americanus* ,,

Johnston's Crocodile, *Tomistoma* (or *Philas*) *johnstoni*   In Case 12
Skull of Gavial, *Gavialis gangeticus* ,,
Alligator, *Alligator mississippiensis* ..   ..   ,,
Indian Rock Snake, *Python molurus*   ..   In Special Case
American Boa, *Boa constrictor,* 16 feet long ..   .. In Case 7

Class V.—PISCES or FISHES.

Port Jackson Shark, *Heterodontus phillipi* ..   .. In Case 11
Torpedo Ray or Numb Fish, *Hypnos subnigerum* ..   In Case 11

Cartilagenous Skeletons of Sharks and Rays   .. In Case 11
Cod, *Oligorus gigas*   .. In Case 7

XIV.

PALÆONTOLOGY or FOSSILS.

THE FOSSIL ORGANIC REMAINS in the Australian Museum are at present arranged in three portions—the Extinct Vertebrata, the Australian Plants and Invertebrata, and a General Foreign Collection.

THE EXTINCT VERTEBRATA are placed in the Osteological Hall in five table cases (Nos. 13 to 17) supplemented by larger objects on pedestals round the hall. The EXTINCT MAMMALIA OF AUSTRALIA take a prominent place in this part of the collection, and include many specimens figured by the veteran Palæontologist Sir Richard Owen, in his remarkable Memoirs on the "Extinct Mammals of Australia." It is now generally accepted that these forerunners of the present Australian Marsupials greatly exceeded the latter in size, and this fact is well demonstrated in the remains now before us.

In one case (No. 14) are bones of Kangaroos from the bone-breccia of the Wellington Valley Caves, placed by Professor Owen in the genera *Palorchestes*, *Procoptodon*, *Protemnodon*, and *Sthenurus*.

The next case (No. 15), to the west of that to which we have just referred, contains the bones of the "Pouched Dog," *Thylacoleo carnifex*, Owen. Unlike the true Kangaroos just mentioned, which were strictly herbivorous, this animal subsisted on flesh. In the same case are also the pelvis and the limb bones of a true *Thylacinus* from Wellington, and the skull of a very large species from the Murrumbidgee Caves at Cave Flat.

Contiguous to the last case, are others (Nos. 16 and 17) containing the remains of the huge *Diprotodon australis*, the largest of the Marsupials, the skull alone measuring three feet in length in full grown individuals. It was herbivorous in habit, is believed to have rivalled the *Rhinoceros* in size, and to be related to the Native Bear or Wombat. Its bones have been found distributed generally throughout Eastern and Southern Australia; and through the researches of the late Edward T. Hardman, Government Geologist of W. Australia, we now know that it attained as great a northerly range as the Lennard River, 80 miles from King Sound (Lat. 17° 20′ S., Long. 125° E.) The specimens include a representation of the large skull now in the Museum of Natural History, London, along with several limb bones, vertebræ, and molar teeth. From the lacustrine deposits of the Darling Downs is a fine pelvis and several caudal vertebræ, the diameter of the pelvic bones being three feet. The similar bones of a still larger individual from Coolah are exhibited, in which the span reached three feet six inches.

Of the allied genus *Nototherium* there are exhibited, in case No. 17, several teeth and the original skull, the most perfect hitherto found of this animal which was named, by the late W. Sharp Macleay, *Zygomaturus*. It was, however, shown by Prof. Sir R. Owen to be identical with his previously described *Nototherium*.

Of the *Phascolomyidæ* or Wombats there are in case No. 14 three remarkable bones representing an individual which must have stood at least four feet high when alive. These consist of humerus, femur and ulna. With these also are strange, flat and broad curved teeth, probably the front upper incisors of a marsupial rodent-like animal, which has been named by Dr. E. P. Ramsay *Sceparnodon*. The teeth in question were found at King's Creek, Darling Downs, and at Lake Eyre, South Australia.

The order *Monotremata*, containing the "Porcupine" (*Echidna*) and the "Platypus" (*Ornithorhynchus*), is represented in the fossil state by a few bones from the Wellington Valley Caves, shown in case No. 14, certainly those of a terrestrial and fossorial genus, and probably identical with the *Echidna*, but greatly larger than the living species. The remains of this order were first found in a fossil state by the late Mr. Gerard Krefft, formerly Curator of this Museum.

In the Central Hall, placed on separate pedestals are casts of the skulls of extinct Indian Elephants. The following are represented :—*Elephas planifrons*, Falc., *E. hysndricus*, and *E. bombifrons*, from the Pliocene beds of the Siwalik Hills, *E. namadicus*, found in the Pliocene deposits of Nerbudda, and *Mastodon ohioticus* from the Post-Tertiary beds of North America. To these there has lately been added a fine cast of the cranium and tusks of another extinct Indian Elephant— *Elephas ganesa*, Falc. and Cautl., taken from the original specimen in the Department of Geology, British Museum, London. Near this is a reproduction of the cranium, mandible, and tusks of the *Elephas antiquus*, Falc., from the Pleistocene deposits of Belgium. The original of this is in the Royal Museum of Natural History of Belgium, at Brussels. Lastly, this series of casts is concluded by that of the *Mastodon humboldti*, Cuvier, from the Pampas Formation (Pleistocene) of Buenos Ayres, Argentine Republic, also taken from the original in the British Museum.

In close contiguity to these is the representation of the skull of one of the *Giraffidæ*, called *Sivatherium*, also from the Siwalik Hills. "It possessed two pairs of horns on its head, two short and simple in front, and two larger palmated ones behind them. From the persistent character of these bony horn-cores we may certainly regard this animal as a gigantic four-horned ruminant, having a resemblance in some structural characters to the Giraffe, in others to the Antelope."

On the large central table will be found a representation of the skull and mandible of an extinct mammal called *Toxodon platensis*, from the Newer Tertiary deposits or Pampas Formation of South America. It was probably larger than a horse, but possessed incisor teeth resembling those of the Rodents.

Again, on the large table is a specimen of the *Megatherium americanum*, or Gigantic Sloth, of South America, a cast taken from the actual remains in the British Museum. "This collossal animal measures 18 feet in length, its bones being more massive than those of the Elephant. The thigh bone is nearly thrice the thickness of the same bone in the largest of existing Elephants, the circumference being equal to the entire length. The strength of the Megatherium is indicated by the form of the bones, with their surfaces, ridges and crests everywhere roughened for the attachment of powerful muscles and tendons. The bony framework of the fore part of the body is comparatively slender, but the hinder quarters display in every part enormous strength and weight combined, indicating that the animal habitually rested on its haunches and powerful tail. Whilst in that position it could freely use its strong flexible forearms and the large claws with which its fore feet were provided to break down or uproot the trees upon the leaves and succulent branches of which it fed, like its pigmy modern representative, the existing Tree Sloth, which spends its entire life climbing back downwards among the branches of the trees. The jaws are destitute of teeth in the front, but there are indications that the snout was elongated, and more or less flexible whilst the fore part of the lower jaw is much prolonged and grooved . . . . . . to give support to a long cylindrical, powerful, muscular tongue, aided by which the great sloth, like the giraffe, could strip off the small branches of the trees, which, by its colossal strength, it had uprooted. In the Elephants, which subsist on similar food to that of the *Megatherium*—the grinding of the food is effected by molar teeth which are replaced by successional ones as the old are worn away. In the Giant Ground Sloth only one set of teeth were provided, but these by constant upward growth, and continual addition of new matter beneath, lasted as long as the animal lived, and never needed renewal . . . . . . Although so much larger in bulk than their modern representative, these huge extinct vegetarians of the New World all belong to one family, being classed with the "Great Ant Eaters" in the order Edentata (or toothless animals), but the Ant-eaters are the only ones in the class that have no teeth, the others having teeth in the sides of their jaws but none in front. At the time when these animals lived in the vast wooded regions through which the upper waters of the Parana and Uruguay flowed, the lowlands, which now forms the great 'pampas' or grassy plains, of the La Plata, were probably submerged estuarine, or delta areas, on which the great rivers annually deposited the fine sediment which they brought down, together with the bodies of *Megatheria, Mylodons, Glyptodons,* &c., drowned during floods in the upper

valleys where they had their habitat.   Hundreds of the fossil
remains of these huge herbivora have been met with in this
pampas formation exposed in the beds of the sluggish rivers
which now traverse these plains."*

The remains of BIRDS in our Palæontological Collection are at
present confined almost exclusively to those of the gigantic wingless bird of New Zealand called the "Moa" (*Dinornis*).   These
occupy cases in the Osteological Hall (Nos. 13 and 8), not far
removed from the Marsupial remains.   No less than eighteen species
of these birds have been described, varying in size from three to
ten feet in height.   The Maori "ovens" have been extensively
searched by the Hon. Walter Mantell and the late Sir Julius von
Haast, and from the bones exhumed, these birds must have formed
a favourite article of diet with the older inhabitants of those
islands.   In the Foreign Collection (to be referred to later) is a
cast of the oldest known bird, the *Archæopteryx macrura*, Owen,
from the Lithographic Stone of Solenhofen, in Bavaria.   The
Collection, however, contains bones of an Emu *(Dromaius)*,
from the Wellington Valley Caves, and the femur of an allied
extinct genus *Dromornis*, Owen, from the Peak Downs, Queensland.

The REPTILIA are at present represented but to a limited extent.   In the order *Crocodilia* the Museum is fortunate enough
to possess the type specimen of the *Mystriosaurus mandelslohi*,
Kaup, from the Lias of Würtemburg.   This reptile may be taken as
a forerunner of the "Gavial" of the Ganges.   The teeth
were similarly long, slender and sharp, and adapted for the prehen-
sion of fishes (Owen).   The sub-order *Thiropoda* (Beast-footed) is
represented by a cast of the head of the *Megalosaurus*, a carnivorous reptile from the chalk of Maestricht, Belgium, placed
against the gallery balustrade in the Geological Hall.   Accom-
panying this are reproductions of several members of the order
Ichythyosauria (Fish Lizards), including *Ichthyosaurus intermedius*,
Conyb., from the Lias of England ; and a portion of the head of a

---

* Guide to the Exhibition Galleries of Geology and Palæontology in the
British Museum, 1884, p. 29.

very large species, in which the size acquired by these reptiles is well exemplified, and also the large orbit with the circlet of sclerotic or bony plates used as a protection to the large eye. Members of this group of reptiles are known to have grown to the great length of twenty-two feet.

The genus *Ichthyosaurus* has been met with in the Mesozoic rocks of Australia and New Zealand ; and in the same case with the *Thylacoleo* remains (No. 15. Osteological Hall), are temporarily placed casts of the bones of *I. australis*, a species described by Prof. McCoy from North Central Queensland. These consist of several vertebræ, portions of the skull showing the bony orbit, a paddle, &c , and are taken from the originals in the National Museum, Melbourne.

The remains of the *Chelonia* (Tortoises and Turtles) have been discovered in the Cave-breccia of Wellington, and fragments of the carapace, probably of a freshwater Turtle are shown in case No. 15 in the Osteological Hall. In this order must now be placed the remarkable heads and disjointed bones known as *Megalania* and *Meiolania*, formerly described by Sir Richard Owen as those of a gigantic horned lizard. So far palæontological research has only revealed the existence of these animals in the Quarternary or Post-Tertiary deposits of Queensland and Lord Howe Island.* The dimensions of the largest, *Meiolania oweni* Smith Woodw. (= *Megalania prisca*, Owen), were fourteen feet or even more in length, with nine horn-like prominences on its tail, which measured one foot ten and a half inches in breadth. "The skull, at first glance, looks like that of some flat-headed form of Ox; but the bones are altogether dissimilar, and the jaws are without teeth." This species is from Queensland, but the Lord Howe Island form is smaller. Representations of the skull of the former, and bony tail sheaths of both species are in the same case with the *Ichthyosaurus* remains (No. 15 Osteological Hall). The carapace of an undoubted Turtle and an egg from the Post-Tertiary deposits of Lord Howe Island, and the head of what will probably prove to be another species of *Meiolania*, have lately been added.

---

* The remains of *Meiolania* are now known to occur in the Pliocene Deep Lead at Canadian Lead, Gulgong.

I

THE GENERAL COLLECTION OF AUSTRALIAN PLANTS AND INVERTEBRATA, is

placed in table-cases at the north end of the Geological Hall, and is at present in a state of transition and re-arrangement.

In the same hall, and contiguous to the latter are two cases of Quaternary Foreign Mammalian bones, both casts and originals. These include skulls of Bear from the Caverne de Goyet, and other caves; antlers of Deer from Post-Pliocene deposits of Anvers, Belgium; jaws of *Rhinoceros* and tusks of *Elephas* from the same place; skull of *Anthracotherium* from Auvergne; and the skull of *Brotherium bombifrons* from Kentucky.

THE GENERAL FOREIGN COLLECTION is

placed in the table cases of the gallery around the Geological Hall. This series is arranged both zoologically and geologically, in order to show the sequence of strata throughout the world, and their typical organic remains. With the view of exemplifying this in the clearest manner the fossils of each formation are placed on differently coloured tablets.

XV.

GEOLOGY AND MINERALOGY.

The Minerals in the Australian Museum are arranged as follows :—

1. General collection of minerals.

2. Collection of wooden models of crystals and natural crystals (as part of the collection illustrating physical characters of minerals.)

3. Collection of meteorites.

4. Ornamental collection—cut stones and imitations.

5. Collection illustrating the physical properties of minerals.

6. Collection illustrating the processes of determination of minerals.

7. Collection illustrating dynamical (viz. : mechanical and chemical) geology.

8. Collection illustrating the modes of occurrence of ores and minerals, including alluvial deposits (mostly New South Wales.)

9. Gold collection (general)

10. Collection of precious stones (general.)

11. Collection of Australasian minerals.

12. Collection of rocks with the Australasian rocks included in parts.

13. Australasian collection arranged according to geological regions, or regional collections.

14. Collection of Italian rocks and minerals.

The "Descriptive Catalogue of the General Collection of Minerals" issued in 1885 is, up to date (1890), the only catalogue of minerals published of late years by the Trustees of the Museum; it will be found useful to students and to visitors, from the amount of information it contains on the subject. There are about 2340 specimens numbered and about 400 which have been purchased since the issue of the catalogue, and not yet numbered; some of them being very remarkable for their size, beauty, or rarity.

I.—GENERAL COLLECTION OF MINERALS.

The arrangement adopted for this collection has been fully explained in the catalogue.

In some systems of mineralogy, prominent importance is given to certain laws based on the proportions of the combined elements, and to the molecular arrangement of these elements in connection with the crystalline form. It is easy to understand, however, that, if this system be adhered to, any particular metal sought for by the practical man is likely to appear in different sections, widely apart from each other, according to the classes of combinations in which it occurs. For instance, Garnierite (the Nickel ore of New Caledonia, which is a silicate), Chrysocolla (silicate of copper), Electric Calamine (silicate of zinc), Rhodonite (silicate of manganese), in such systems, are distributed in different groups among the Silicates; while in the system adopted here, these minerals will be found respectively in the Nickel class, in the Copper class, in the Zinc class, and in the Manganese class among the Metallic Minerals. It does not always follow, however, that the mineral considered should be a workable ore of the metal in which class it has been placed. Sulphide of Iron, or Iron Pyrites, is worked for gold and for sulphur, but not for iron; still it belongs to the Iron class. Whenever it has been found convenient to represent an important mineral in more than one class, it has been done.

The minerals are divided into two main sections (see Catalogue, pages 9 to 12), viz. :—

I.—Non-metallic minerals, placed on the left hand side of the room.

II.—Metallic minerals, placed on the right hand side of the room.

NON-METALLIC MINERALS.

The order of sequence into which the so-called rocks, or non-metallic minerals are arranged, is as follows :—

Carbon class, including Diamond (see precious stones) Graphite (Plumbago or black lead), Coal, Oil Shales, Amber, &c.

Boron class, including Boron, &c.

Sulphur class ; Ex. Sulphur found in volcanic districts.

Alkaline and Earthy Minerals, divided into :

1. Alkaline salts ; Ex. Rock Salt, &c.

2. Alkaline earthy salts; Ex. Calcite, Aragonite (Carbonate of Lime, or Limestone), Selenite (Sulphate of Lime, or Gypsum), Apatite (Phosphate of Lime), Fluor-Spar, &c.

3. Alumina and Aluminates ; Ex. Corundum, including Sapphire and Ruby (composed of alumina), Spinel Ruby (an aluminate of magnesia), &c. Emery is impure corundum mixed with oxide of iron. (See Catalogue pages 1 to 38, Nos. 1 to 433.)

Silica and Hydrous Silica ; Ex. Quartz (including Rock Crystal, Amethyst, Agate, Flint, Jasper, &c.). Opal is hydrous silica, or silica containing water. (See Catalogue, pages 39 to 44, Nos. 434 to 574.)

Silicates proper, including the more important groups, namely :

1. Pyroxene group ; Ex. Augite, &c., found in basalt and other eruptive rocks.

2. Amphibole group ; Ex. Hornblende, Asbestos, &c., occurring chiefly in schists and eruptive rocks.

3. Olivine group ; Ex. Olivine or Peridot, a bottle-green gem found in basalt.

4. Garnet group ; The red variety is a common gem.

5. Epidote group; Ex. Epidote, a dark green mineral, which is sometimes good enough to cut for a gem.

6. Mica group; This affords a transparent and tough substitute for glass, and is used in stoves and lamps.

7. Talc group; Ex. Steatite, Figure stone, &c.

8. Sepiolite group; Ex. Sepiolite (Meerschaum).

9. Serpentine group; Affords pretty ornamental stones when polished.

10. Chlorite group; Ex. Chlorite, a mica-like mineral found in some schists and other rocks.

11. Felspar group; An extensive group including:—

Orthoclase, one of the components of granite. Moonstone, Sunstone, Amazonstone are varieties of the same.

Labradorite and Oligoclase, which occur in many eruptive and volcanic rocks.

12. Andalusite group; Ex. Chiastolite or Mascle, Cyanite, a beautiful blue semi-precious stone.

13. Staurolite group; Ex. Staurolite, or Cross Stone.

Silicates containing other Acids (Boracic Acid, Hydrofluoric Acid, Hydrochloric Acid, Sulphuric Acid), besides Silicic Acid, including as principal groups :—

1. Datolite group; Ex. Datolite, Danburite.
2. Axinite group; Ex. Axinite, crystals in the shape of axe-heads.

3. Tourmaline group; Ex. Tourmaline, often in company with stream tin.

4. Topaz group; Ex. Topaz, blue, white, and yellow varieties.

5. Ultramarine group; Ex. Ultramarine, or Lapis Lazuli, affording a beautiful ornamental stone and a rich blue pigment, which is also manufactured artificially. (See Catalogue pages 89 to 44, Nos. 1055 to 1105.)

Silicates with Glucina, including Emerald, a rich green precious stone, and Beryl or Aquamarine.

Silicates with Zirconia, including Zircon, a rather disregarded gem, very common in drift and often mistaken for ruby tin. (See Catalogue pages 94 to 97, Nos. 1106 to 1132.)

The Zeolites, including several groups of beautifully crystallized minerals occurring chiefly in basalts.

Clay group; An important and useful group; Ex. Common Clay, Pipe Clay, Fire Clay, Kaolin, etc. (See Catalogue, pages 49 to 89, Nos. 575 to 1054.)

When specimens included in the above subdivisions have been found too large to be displayed in the flat show-cases, they have been placed in special cases.

METALLIC MINERALS.

The classes into which the metallic minerals have been divided will be found in the cases in the following order:

Zinc, Manganese, Iron, Cobalt, Nickel, Meteorites (debris of planets described further on as a special collection), Tin, Titanium, Chromium, Molybdenum, Tungsten (Wolfram, &c.), Uranium, Arsenic, Antimony, Bismuth, Lead, Copper, Mercury, Silver, Gold, Tellurium and Selenium, Platinum and other rare metals of the Platinum class. The two metalloids, Tellurium and Selenium, which belong chemically to the Sulphur class, are very rare, but are placed here as an appendix to gold and silver, with either or both of which they are sometimes found associated or combined, as well as with lead and bismuth. (See Catalogue pages 105 to 206, Nos. 1161 to 2340).

Next come the minerals which are mostly found in the rock called Zircon-Syenite, and containing the rare metals Yttrium, Cerium, Thorium, Tantalum, Columbium, Zirconium, &c. (See Catalogue pages 98 to 103, Nos. 1133 to 1160.)

NEW PURCHASES (NOT CATALOGUED).

Among the Minerals which have been purchased between 1887 and 1889 and which are not included in the catalogue, the following are the most remarkable :—

As examples of large crystals :—Barytes from Cumberland, and Whitherite from Alston Moore, England ; Orthoclase and Wernerite, both from Renfrew, Canada ; Garnet, three inches along diagonal, from Salides, Colorado ; Rhodonite, Willemite, and Franklinite, from Franklin, New Jersey.

Opposite the large blocks of Malachite, on the top shelf of the upright case, is a specimen of Muscovite (Mica) from Mitchell County, North Carolina showing, when closely examined, some hexagonal figures of crystallization.

The following remarkable minerals will be found in the general collection placed according to their class :—Turquoise from New Mexico ; Chlorite, a pseudomorph after Garnet from Ishpening, Michigan ; Wulfenite from Nevada ; Descloizite and Vanadinite from southern Arizona ; Malachite with Azurite, and a stalactite of Malachite from Arizona ; Electrum (an alloy of gold and silver containing 30 per cent. of the last metal), crystallized in the shape of the plant called Liver-wort, from Hungary.

In the Tellurium and Selenium classes the following may be mentioned :—Sylvanite, a Telluride of Gold and Silver, from Hungary ; Tellurium from Colorado, placed close to the same metal (Catalogue No. 2042) from Transylvania ; a Selenide of Bismuth, Guanajuatite, from Mexico ; this is a rare mineral of a bluish-grey colour with metallic lustre.

Another interesting mineral of Bismuth, which differs from the above in composition, on account of the presence of Tellurium instead of Selenium, is Tetradymite, which will be found in the Catalogue No. 1651 in the Bismuth class. This mineral is of a pale steel-grey colour, resplendent with metallic lustre, is from Retzbanya, Hungary, and is the more interesting on account of its having also been discovered in New South Wales. It has been recently analysed and identified by Mr. Mingaye of the Department of Mines.

Roscoelite is a mineral which deserves special mention. It is composed of Silica, Vanadic acid, Alumina, Potash, &c., and occurs in dark minute scales like Mica ; it is from Granite Creek, near Coloma, El Dorado County, California, where it occurs intimately mixed with gold in small seams in porphyry. Its composition and its association with that metal are remarkable, and it has been provisionally placed in the case containing specimens of Gold.

A collection of Gold and Silver Ores and a collection of Meteorites purchased in 1888 with some other well known minerals will be found in their respective subdivisions.

II.—COLLECTION OF WOODEN MODELS OF CRYSTALS AND CRYSTALLIZED MINERALS.

This collection occupies the two large central show cases; it consists of 743 wooden models arranged according to the six systems of Crystallography, namely: Cubic, Tetragonal, Hexagonal, Rhombic, Oblique, and Triclinic or Asymmetric.

In order to make this collection useful and interesting, even to those unacquainted with the subject, the faces of the models have been painted in colours to show the different forms, which are usually found combined in each system in a more or less complicated manner.

For instance, in the Cubic System, a simple form, the Octahedron, is painted white on its eight faces, so that, considering only the holohedral forms on the left side of the tray, every complex form in which the octahedron enters into combination with other forms, will be known at a glance, and so on for others; while the models of the simple ones, eight in number, will be easily distinguished by being of only one colour.

On the right side of the tray are placed the models of hemihedral forms, so-called because they have only half the number of faces of the corresponding holohedral forms, the simplest being the Tetrahedron, of four faces, corresponding to the Octahedron.

This collection of models has been illustrated by good examples of natural crystals, which are placed in the same tray as the crystallographic system to which they respectively belong. For other examples of crystals the visitor (especially by using the Catalogue) can refer to the general collection, where well crystallized minerals will be found.

In the first tray (Cubic System) the following crystallized minerals are represented, Diamond (a cube from Brazil), Fluor Spar, Pleonaste or Black Spinel, Spinel Ruby, Garnet, Zincblende, Magnetic Iron, Pyrite, Cobaltite, Galena, Red Oxide of Copper, Argentite or Silver Glance, and Gold (an Octahedron with some faces of the cube).

In the second tray (Tetragonal System), Tin ore or Cassiterite, and Zircon are represented.

In the third tray (Hexagonal System) will be found Carbonate of Lime or Calcite, a mineral which occurs in the greatest variety of forms and combinations. Phosphate of Lime or Apatite, Corundum, Quartz, Tourmaline, and Beryl, or Aquamarine are also exhibited.

On the other side, in the fourth tray, the Rhombic System is illustrated by the following crystallized minerals :—Heavy Spar, also known as Sulphate of Baryta or Barytes, Celestite or sulphate of strontia, Aragonite and Calcite, both carbonates of lime, Anhydrite, Olivine, Pinite, Staurolite, Topaz, Manganite, Stibnite (antimony ore), Mispikel, Redruthite (copper glance), Stephanite (brittle silver), &c.

In the fifth tray the Oblique System is illustrated by Borax, Gypsum, Augite, Diopside, Hornblende, Epidote, Orthoclase, Felspar, Hormotome, Datolite, Titanite, and Azurite (blue carbonate of copper). In the same tray the Triclinic System is illustrated by Cryolite, Microcline, Albite, Oligoclase, Anorthite, Labradorite, and Cyanite.

The last tray contains a selection of large crystals by which the six Crystallographic Systems are again illustrated.

In two special cases are exhibited two gigantic hexagonal crystals, one of Apatite (phosphate of lime), the other of Beryl or Aquamarine, the latter measuring fourteen inches in height and one foot along the diagonal of the base.

III.—COLLECTION OF METEORITES.

The Meteorites are kept in a special case next to the metal Nickel, which most of them contain. In course of time they will form a larger and more systematic collection, although the specimens are not very numerous as yet. Among them will be found a cast of the Deniliquin or Baratta Meteorite, the original of which is in possession of Mr. Russell, Government Astronomer, and weighs 145 lbs.; it has a specific gravity of 3·387 and is mostly composed of the minerals Enstatite, Olivine, and Nickeliferous Iron. Professor Liversidge read two papers on it, which are published in the Journals of the Royal Society of New South Wales, 1872 and 1882. This example shows that Meteorites are not all metal, some, indeed being true rocks like our dyke-rocks, while others contain carbon.

An interesting fact connected with the metallic Meteorites, or more correctly the metallic part of some of them, is the crystallization which is brought out by polishing a section of the specimen and using acid on the surface. Of the different alloys of nickel and iron which enter into the composition of these Meteorites, one is more easily attacked by the acid than the other, the result being the production of the figures of crystallization. These can be seen in the specimens exhibited, one from Augusta County, Virginia, one from Tolucca, Mexico, and another from Port Duncan, Texas, the dates of their fall being unknown.

The largest metallic Meteorite known is one over three tons in weight, which was found in Victoria, and is now in the British Museum.

Still more interesting than the above are the stony Meteorites, some of which are identical with the deep rocks of our globe. Most of them contain the mineral Olivine or Peridot, and belong to the family of rocks called Peridotites, while some others are true volcanic rocks. Intermediate between the metallic Meteorites, and the stony Meteorites are some containing the characteristics of both.

The analogy between these and the rocks of our planet is carried out in all the details of their structure, some being fragmentary like our breccias, some oolitic, some granular like sandstone, while others exhibit structures peculiar to some volcanic rocks, being vascular, globular, vitreous, &c., leaving no doubt that they are the debris of a small disintegrated satellite of the earth.

IV.—ORNAMENTAL COLLECTION.

With the exception of some nicely cut vases of Fluor Spar, placed in a special case at the entrance of the room, one ornamental vase of Porphyry, and two of Serpentine exhibited by themselves, and some Marble and Serpentine slabs along the wall, most of the ornamental stones are placed in an upright case standing opposite the entrance.

Among the stones or non-metallic minerals the principal mineralogical specimens represented are Calcite and Aragonite (Carbonate of Lime) represented by Slabs of Onyx, Marbles, and a small "sarcophagus" of rare antique marble. The material from which some candlesticks and vases exhibited under Catalogue numbers 2243 to 2249 are made, although known as alabaster is not *true* alabaster, which is a variety of Gypsum (sulphate of lime), but is a variety of concretionary marble analogous to the stalactites of limestone caves. A variety of true Alabaster (another sulphate of lime) also called Satin Spar is represented by a necklace and cross under No. 2242. The name of Satin Spar, as well as Alabaster, has been given to varieties of both Sulphate and Carbonate of Lime, a specimen of the latter being in the general collection under No. 199. Silicic Acid or Silica includes here the numerous ornamental varieties of quartz, and impure quartz of different colors such as Agate, Onyx, Jasper, Chrysoprase, &c. In order to mark a striking distinction between the different varieties of quartz, which are considered as gems, such as Amethyst, Smoky Quartz, Cairngorm, Citrine Quartz, &c., and the other gems, among which are the most precious stones, the large collection of cut amethysts has been placed in this case.

Among the silicates are Figure-stone or Agalmatolite, and the precious Jade, from both of which many Chinese ornaments and other articles are made. Serpentine is the material of the carved stone representing two serpents in allusion to the origin of the name. Catlinite, a red clay rock, is the material of an Indian pipe from Minnesota.

Among the metallic minerals, a few are represented here by cut ornaments; namely, Rhodonite (Silicate of Manganese), Hematite (Oxide of Iron), and Malachite (Carbonate of Copper). A large slab of Chalcedony from Italy, which has been framed as the top of a table, is a good example of concretionary structure.

In the most southerly of the cases on the right side of the room, the rest of the ornamental and semi-precious stones, as well as some models and imitations, rough uncut gems and samples of gem sand, &c., are displayed.

The space in the cases between the last mentioned and the last case containing the minerals of the rare metals Yttrium, Cerium, &c., is left vacant to receive provisionally, recently acquired specimens.

Against the south wall in the centre, rich blocks of Malachite in geodes from Peak Downs, Queensland, are exhibited in a special case, showing beautiful velvety crystallizations.

V.—COLLECTION ILLUSTRATING THE PHYSICAL PROPERTIES OF MINERALS.

This collection will be found useful to beginners and persons unacquainted with the terms of Mineralogy.

The form is first examined : (1) Geometric by crystallization. Ex.: Rock Crystal or Quartz. (2) Geometric by contraction. Ex. : Prisms of Basalt, Sandstone, &c. On the other hand, when it is irregular, accidental or imitative, the form is indeterminate. Some minerals exhibiting indeterminate forms may be crystalline in structure, while others are not so. Of these forms examples of concretions, incrustations and weathering are shown. A perfectly rounded ball of sandstone from near Carcoar, is a rather puzzling specimen. It has evidently been produced by a mechanical though natural, mode of weathering, such as would be the case in a hole under a waterfall, where the process of whirling has been kept on for centuries.

The different modes of structure are exhibited, namely— granular, lamellar, fibrous, radiate, concretionary, dendritic, earthy, vitreous, &c. These expressions are always used in the description of minerals, and the specimens exhibited afford some points of comparison.

When a mineral is freshly broken the fracture is sometimes a very good means of determination. In crystallized minerals it is either irregular, or takes place along certain planes, which are called planes of cleavage. Iceland Spar (Calcite) is a good instance of three perfect and easy cleavages. Some crystallized minerals, however, exhibit a curved surface when broken, and such fracture is called conchoidal; the best examples of conchoidal fracture are given by vitreous, and some more or less homogeneous minerals. Ex. : Volcanic Glass, Flint, and Kerosene Shale.

On handling minerals certain mechanical properties are manifested by tests, which also serve to distinguish them. Hardness is thus an important character. In order to find an easy definition of the degree of hardness of a mineral it is compared with some other minerals which are considered as standards, and are known by numbers representing the degree of hardness. The list thus formed is called the scale of hardness. It is arranged as follows :—

1. Talc.
2. Gypsum. } Scratched by the nail.
3. Calcite.
4. Fluor Spar. } Scratched by a steel point.
5. Apatite.
6. Orthoclase. Scratches glass.
7. Quartz.
8. Topaz.
9. Corundum.
10. Diamond. The hardest of all known substances.

Silver Glance (**Argentite**) is a very good example o malleability; this mineral acts like lead when cut with a knife. Flexibility and elasticity are well exemplified by Mica and Flexible Sandstone. Of the latter two varieties are known, one from Brazil, the other from North Carolina.

Another class of properties of minerals includes those which fall under the sense of sight, as transparency, Ex.: Limpid Quartz; translucency, Ex.: Cloudy Quartz. Lustre and colour are two important characteristics by which many minerals can be known at a glance. Lustre is either metallic, Ex.: Gold, Iron Pyrites; adamantine, Ex.: Diamond, Carbonate of Lead; resinous, Ex.: Realgar; silky, Ex.: Satin Spar; or vitreous, Ex.: Quartz. Minerals which exhibit metallic or adamantine lustre are, in general, heavy. There are some minerals of which the colour is characteristic, Ex.: Malachite, green. There are others which occur of different colours, Ex.: Corundum, red (Ruby), blue (Sapphire), green (Oriental emerald), purple (Oriental amethyst).

VI.—COLLECTION ILLUSTRATING DETERMINATION OF MINERALS.

Under this title is a collection, the object of which is to illustrate some simple processes of testing, by exhibiting the most common minerals which answer to the tests.

First of all a ready distinction is made between minerals possessing, or not possessing a metallic lustre. Hence two classes. The minerals exhibiting a metallic lustre are divided into two groups according to their resistance and fusibility under the blowpipe. The first group includes minerals which are easily fusible or volatile, and leads to minor subdivisions, the principal of which are characterised by the presence or absence of sulphur antimony, arsenic or tellurium, as shown by a careful use of the blowpipe. A great number of well-known ores are identified by these tests. The second group includes minerals which are infusible, or fuse with difficulty and give a magnetic mass after being heated under the blowpipe. It includes several ores of iron, chrome, &c.

The minerals which do not exhibit a metallic lustre are divided into three groups. The first includes minerals which burn or volatilize easily under the blowpipe, such as Sulphur, Cinnabar, Oxide of Antimony, &c. The second includes minerals which melt more or less easily, but do not disappear by volatilization under ordinary circumstances, such as Chloride of Silver, Carbonate of Lead, Malachite, Garnet, Tourmaline, &c. The third includes minerals which are infusible or only fusible with difficulty, such as Quartz and many silicates and gems, some Iron ores, many earthy minerals, Limestone, Chrome ore, Pitchblende, Tin ore, Zincblende, Nickel ore (Garnierite), &c. Some of them appear in two groups.

The scale of fusibility affords some means of comparison, and the degree of fusibility is expressed by a number It is arranged as follows :—

1. Stibnite. Fuses easily in the candle flame.
2. Natrolite. Fuses in the candle flame.
3. Almandine Garnet. Fuses easily before the blowpipe.
4. Actinolite, a variety of Hornblende. Fuses more or less easily before the blowpipe when in minute fragments.
5. Adularia. A variety of Orthoclase.
6. Bronzite. Small fragments are only rounded on the edges before the blowpipe.
7. Quartz. Infusible in ordinary blowpipe flame.

VII.—COLLECTION ILLUSTRATING DYNAMICAL GEOLOGY.

This collection, though but recently commenced, is one that will commend itself to the student and miner. It is difficult to trace strict divisions, but, broadly speaking, there are phenomena taking place both on the surface and at various depths, which are rather to be classed as mechanical than otherwise, and there are phenomena in which chemical actions are predominant.

Among the results of mechanical action, examples are exhibited illustrating the effects of such pressures as cause the cleavages of rocks, the wedged ends of faulted reefs, &c., the results of earth movements in metalliferous lodes.

The effect of chemical action, sometimes combined with physical action such as heat, is exemplified by the decomposition of minerals and rocks, the deposition of minerals from solutions, the change of minerals into other minerals, or pseudomorphism, the change of rocks into other rocks, or metamorphism, &c.

This collection, which is rapidly being increased, has recently received specimens illustrating phenomena of considerable interest as contributions to the puzzling questions of the formation of minerals and mineral veins. These tend to show that in some mineral veins in which quartz apparently stands alone as the usual matrix of gold, carbonate of lime was formerly the matrix, but has been removed in solution leaving quartz and gold only, or in some instances has been replaced by quartz as a pseudomorph.

To this collection are appended, as illustrating part of Chemical Geology, some specimens of artificially formed minerals such as boiler deposits, furnace products, stalactites and stalagmites formed from building materials, spring deposits, &c.

VIII.—COLLECTION ILLUSTRATING THE MODES OF OCCURRENCE OF MINERALS.

Although the Museum possesses a large general collection of minerals, which can be examined by students of mineralogy, it has been found profitable, in the interest of mining students, to exhibit the ores and valuable products of Australia, in such a manner as to give a recognised individuality to what is called a *mineral* deposit or an *ore* deposit. Thus, when possible, the ores have been accompanied by specimens of the local rocks, specimens of eruptive rocks occuring in or near the deposit, and specimens of minerals found in close association with the ores. This mode, no doubt, will command the attention of the mining community from an educational point of view.

IX.—COLLECTION OF GOLD SPECIMENS.

The collection of Alluvial Gold includes a number of models of large nuggets for which the colony of Victoria is well known. The largest represented is the " Welcome " (2,195 ozs.), of an approximate value of £8,780, found at a depth of 180 feet

J

at Bakery Hill, Ballaarat, 11th of June, 1858. This is not, however, the largest on record, as in 1869 another, the "Welcome Stranger," of a value of £9,534 (over 2,280 ozs. when found), was unearthed at Dunolly, a locality where countless smaller nuggets have been found.* Next in weight come the "Precious" (1,717 ozs. gross weight), and Viscount Canterbury (1,121 ozs.), both found at Berlin, Victoria.

New South Wales has not so many recorded nuggets. The largest masses of gold found in this colony are: Doctor Kerr's so called "Hundredweight Nugget," found by a native in 1851, at Meroo Creek, Turon River ; and a hundredweight of gold blasted at one time by Beyer and Holtermann at Hawkins Hill in 1873.

A list of the nuggets found in New South Wales is given in Professor Liversidge's "Minerals of New South Wales." From this list it can be seen that numerous nuggets, especially from Kiandra, have been melted without models having been taken of them. Those represented in the Museum which are not in that list are: one from Gulgong, with the shape of a hook at one end ; one from Temora (161 ozs.), found in 1884 ; two from Cadia, near Orange (60 and 32 ozs.) The last has been named the "Ly-ee-moon," having been given to the wreck fund by its owner, Mr. H. W. Newman, of Lucknow. The "Maitland Bar Nugget" is a magnificent specimen, showing quartz and crystals of gold. It was found in 1877, at a depth of five feet, and is valued at £1,236.

Besides the models of nuggets, alluvial gold is represented by a collection of over fifty specimens from New South Wales. Gold from granite regions is in general scaly.

Gold in quartz is shown from Victoria, New South Wales, Queensland, New Zealand, South Australia, and Tasmania ; gold in calcite from Lucknow, Tea-tree (south of Barraba), Tuena, in New South Wales, and from the Transvaal, South Africa.

Specimens of dendritic gold in serpentine and in mispikel (arsenical pyrites), from Lucknow and dendritic gold from New Caledonia are also exhibited.

---

* R. Brough Smyth, Goldfields of Victoria, 1869, p. 600.

Among the minerals which accompany gold at Sandhurst, Victoria, crystals of carbonate of lime and carbonate of iron are prominent. The latter, or Siderite, is represented by a remarkable group of three saddle-shaped crystals, which may be considered as a unique instance, and is described in Vol. X., part 4, of the "Proceedings of the Linnean Society of New South Wales."

As a special collection has been formed comprising gold speci-mens, and as the specimens of this metal from other parts of the world than Australia are not numerous, part of them will be found in the special gold collection, and a few in the general collection. Among those from various parts of the world are gold specimens from England, Scotland, Ireland, Sweden, France, Germany, Bohemia, Hungary, Russia, India, South Africa, North and South America, including Brazil, Peru, &c.

X.—COLLECTION OF PRECIOUS STONES.

In the centre, where the gold is, the collection of Precious Stones from different parts of the world and from Australia has also been placed.

This collection includes a few black Diamonds and Carbonado used for boring rocks with the diamond drill.

A Diamond in its matrix from South Africa forms the most interesting piece in the collection, as nowhere else has diamond yet been found under similar circumstances. The matrix, which fills some large pipe-shaped cavities, contains a great number of minerals, such as olivine, garnet, diallage, &c., which enter ordinarily into the composition of the so-called hydrothermal rocks, besides some debris of the adjacent formation. According to the best authorities such deposits will continue to consider-able depths.

Diamonds, Sapphires, Blue Topaz, and Zircons from New South Wales will be examined with interest by the gold and tin miner, as they may be found in the dish along with those metals.

XI.—COLLECTION OF AUSTRALASIAN MINERALS.

As in the general collection of minerals in the upper floor, this collection commences with coal and is continued with the other non-metallic minerals, followed by the metallic minerals, gold forming a special collection.

NON-METALLIC MINERALS.

The non-metallic minerals are represented specially by Coal from New South Wales; Sulphur from New Zealand; some Marbles from New South Wales; Fire-clays; a crystal of Amethyst from Bolton Vale, 17 miles from Bathurst; a large crystal of Quartz from George's Plain (?); some Zeolites in basalt from Ben Lomond, New England; crystals of Axinite from Moonbi, New England; blue and green Aquamarine or Beryl in a silicious deposit from the Gulf, Vegetable Creek; and some Opals from Queensland.

METALLIC MINERALS OTHER THAN GOLD OR SILVER.

The ores of copper, bismuth, antimony, chromium, tin, nickel, cobalt, iron, and manganese are examined in succession with the peculiar rocks and formations in which they occur; Copper in micaschist, slate, amygdaloid, &c.; Chrome ore in olivine rocks and serpentine; Tin in granite and greisen (a variety of granite); Nickel ore in serpentine, &c.

The silver fields of New South Wales are not yet fully illustrated, but Broken Hill, Sunny Corner, Lewis Ponds, &c., are represented by some of their peculiar ores, including Chloro-Bromide of Silver from Broken Hill. A specimen from Lewis Ponds shows Chloride of Silver with coralloidal structure and moss gold. Stalactites of silver gossan of a delicate texture, comparable to the most elaborate embroidery are shown from the Bulga, near Orange; also some stalactites from Sunny Corner.

XII.—COLLECTION OF ROCKS.

The rocks, though unattractive, are of considerable interest to the miner and to the agriculturist. The former requires a knowledge of rocks which are favourable to the existence of valuable ores, the latter of those which, by their decomposition and disintegration, are capable of producing fertile soils. It is also by studying the rocks that the architect becomes acquainted with the properties of building materials, their resistance to weathering, &c., and the manufacturer with the elements of useful or new materials such as bricks, artificial stones, &c.

The general collection, regarded as a standard collection, will serve as a comparison between the rocks of New South Wales, which are yet sparingly represented, and the typical rocks shown from different parts of the world. In each class the Australian rocks will be found intercalated after the types and arranged in groups by themselves.

Two large subdivisions have been adopted. The sedimentary rocks which occur in strata, the most ancient of which are frequently upturned and much contorted, as well as metamorphosed ; and the eruptive rocks which occur as bosses, dykes, volcanic lavas, &c.

In the sedimentary series are found the Micaschists, Slates, Sandstones, Conglomerates, Breccias, Limestones, Gravels, &c. Fossils are often seen in them.

The eruptive series deserve a close study for various reasons. They have often been associated with great disturbances in the strata of the sedimentary rocks, and some of them have played an important part in the filling of mineral veins, and they contain various crystallized minerals. They can be divided into three broadly defined groups, which must be understood to merge into one another. The Acidic rocks, which contain a large proportion of silica or quartz, Ex. : Granite ; the Basic rocks which contain the least quantity of silica, and consequently the largest amount of bases or oxides, some of these being metallic oxides, such as iron, which give to the generality of these rocks a dark colour, Ex. : Basalt ; between these two extremes and connecting them are the so-called Intermediate rocks, containing in general, less silica than the Acid, and more silica than the Basic rocks, Ex. : Syenite.

XIII.—REGIONAL COLLECTION.

This collection, which is in course of formation, may become of considerable interest to people inhabiting or visiting the Colony of New South Wales. It is intended to show, in a broad sense, the mineralogical and geological constitution of tracts of country, so that the visitor can refer at once to the region in which he feels interested. The divisions adopted include each a certain number of counties, and, as far as possible, are characterized by a predominating geological formation. Ex.: New England, or the Granitic Region of the north; the Hunter River District or Northern Coalfields, &c. The specimens which are required for the formation and improvement of this collection are :—The most characteristic, sedimentary and eruptive rocks, to which the so-called region owes its prominent features, its soil, either rich or poor, and the mineral products which are found abundantly in the district, or occur as a peculiarity of special interest. Some of the sedimentary rocks are rendered more interesting when they contain fossils, a few of which are sufficient to determine the age of the formation.

XIV.—COLLECTION OF ITALIAN ROCKS AND MINERALS.

The oldest members of the series represented have been identified with some of the formations recognized in America, such as the Saint-Alban System, to which the celebrated Carrara marble belongs, in Italy. The most recent rocks represented in this collection include some ancient and recent lavas from Vesuvius.

XVI.

ANTHROPOLOGY AND ETHNOLOGY.

ANTHROPOLOGY (from the Greek *anthrōpos*, man) is the science which treats of our knowledge of the human race. As an animal, man belongs to the Sub-Kingdom Vertebrata, and the Class Mammalia. (See pages 15 and 20.) Viewed in this light, he is represented in the Museum by the series of skeletons and skulls already referred to, but he has also to be considered in relation to his history and development. This section of the subject is known as Ethnology, but only the Ethnology of Australia and the adjacent islands is represented.

The Ethnological specimens are exhibited in a hall recently opened under the name of the " Ethnological Hall," a room about 70 feet long by 30 feet broad, which is entered from the Osteo-logical Hall. The arrangement adopted is mainly geographical — that is, articles from each island or group are placed, as far as possible, in the same or in adjoining cases. Specimens from Australia, New Zealand, and New Guinea are in the gallery, while those from the Islands generally are in cases on the ground floor. A few Egyptian, European, and American specimens are placed in the gallery for comparison, and some interesting relics are in table cases on the ground floor.

On entering the Hall the visitor is recommended to turn to the right and examine the collections in the order of the numbers on the cases.

THE ADMIRALITY ISLANDS are represented by speci-mens in Case No. 1. The most remarkable are Obsidian (or volcanic glass) Spears and Spear Racks, ornamented Adze Handles, Bracelets and Armlets made of trochus shells, Dresses and portions of large Canoe Masts. There are some large Drums suspended from the ceiling above the gallery ; above some

of the cases in the gallery are Oil Jars and Food Bowls, and in
the corner at the top of the stairs is a pile of Food Bowls each
hewn out of solid timber.

THE SOLOMON ISLANDS are next illustrated by exhibits
in Cases Nos. 2, 3 and 4, amongst which are Fishing Floats, Trade
Axes with long handles ornamented with pearl shell, Women's
Dresses, Combs, Shell Armlets, Clubs ornamented with coloured
grasses, Breast Ornaments made of shell, Waist Belts, Arrows,
Ornaments with carvings, three Shields—one ornamented with
shell, one of carved wood, and one of woven cane,—and numerous
small Trinkets of various kinds.   Above centre Cases Nos. 13,
14 and 16 there are Food Bowls ornamented with pearl shell.
Suspended   from   the   ceiling   are   Canoes,   and   the   pillars
supporting the gallery are ornamented with Spears from this
group.   The northern wall in the gallery is decorated with fine
Clubs made by the natives.   In table Case No. 7 in the gallery is
a collection of Stone Axes from Ugi Island.

THE SAMOAN ISLANDS AND TONGA are represented
in Case No. 5 and on the north end wall of the gallery by Tappa
Cloth, Fans, Cloaks made of fibre, and Mat Sulus or Women's
Dresses; and by Stone Implements in table Case No. 7 in
the gallery.

THE VITI OR FIJI ISLANDS specimens are shown
in Case No. 6.   Among them are Women's Dresses, Sleeping
Mats, single and double Pillows, Wigs, Food Baskets, Stone
Adzes, large and small Cava Bowls, Fly Brushes made from
reeds and the tail feathers of the tropic bird, Combs, &c.   Some
Dresses are suspended from the gallery, and on the end wall of the
gallery are large Spears and Clubs.

From ROTUMAH AND FIJI there are also some fine specimens
of printed Tappa Cloth, and large Grass Mats in Case No. 11
(at foot of stairs).

THE NEW HEBRIDES AND NEW CALEDONIA are
illustrated by specimens in Case No. 7.   There are exhibited here
a large flat wooden Figure of a Woman, a small Model of a

Man made from cocoa-nut fibre and clay, Idols made from coral, poisoned Arrows, heavy Spears barbed with human bone, Clubs, Baskets, Food Bowls, a New Caledonian Mask made to represent a Frenchman, hand Clubs, Adzes, Calabashes or Gourds ornamented with cocoa-nut fibre, and used for carrying or taking cocoa-nut oil to the trader. There are also a large Net from New Caledonia and some Dresses from the New Hebrides hanging from the gallery.

A COLLECTION OF CASTS OF HEADS AND FACES of races inhabiting the Islands of the Pacific and the Malay Archipelago is shown in Cases Nos. 8 and 9. This collection was prepared by Dr. Finsch, of Bremen, who spent many years investigating the characteristics of the natives of these islands. A list of the casts forming the collection is to be seen in the cases.

SOUTH AFRICAN SPECIMENS are in Case No. 10. They consist of Trade Shields made from hide, Assegais, Bows, Bags, Baskets, Pipes, Pillows, Chief's Staff, a Blanket made in England for the Zulus, and some Trinkets.

THE NEW IRELAND GROUP OF ISLANDS is represented in Case No. 12 by splendid Wood Carvings of men, birds, shell, and fish, some with long handles; these are used by the natives in their dances. There are also in this case long handled Tomahawks ornamented with beads and coloured grasses, Head Dresses made from the teeth of dogs and other animals, Wigs, Bamboo Flutes ornamenned by lines burnt into the wood, small Fishing Nets, &c. Spears from these islands are arranged round the pillars supporting the gallery, and Clubs are on the walls over the cases and on the stairs. One of the windows at the top of the stairs is filled with Spears made of palm wood with shafts of carved bamboo.

NEW BRITAIN is represented by numerous articles for domestic use in Case No. 12 and by Clubs, Spears, and Paddles on the walls over cases in the gallery and on the stairs.

A COLLECTION OF MASKS, from various islands, representing birds and human beings, with half masks made from human skulls, is exhibited in the large centre Cases Nos. 13 and 14. These Masks are used for ceremonial dances and religious ceremonies.

THE MORTLOCK ISLAND specimens are in centre Cases Nos. 15 and 16. They consist of fine Native Dress Matting, Pillows, Fish and Shark Hooks, and Adzes made from the shell of *Tridacna gigas* and *Terebra maculata*.

THE MARSHALL ISLANDS specimens are in the same cases. Some of the finest workmanship of any of the South Sea Islands comes from this group. Attention should be given to the Dress Matting, Fishing Lines and Hooks, Hats made from grass and fibre, Swords with the cutting edge of sharks' teeth, a Coat of Armour made from cocoa-nut fibre. From RAPANUI or EASTER ISLAND there are Wooden Idols, a large State Stool, and Fishing Hooks and Lines. And from the HARVEY ISLANDS some splendid ornamented Adzes with carved handles.

In the gallery the most convenient method of obtaining a general view of the collections will be to examine the wall cases, commencing at the head of the stairs, and then to inspect the table cases on the balustrade.

THE BRITISH NEW GUINEA exhibits are arranged in the wall Cases commencing at No. 17. There is in this case a large collection of Pipes made from bamboo, Adzes, Axes, Dresses, Drums, Necklaces made of wallaby's teeth, Cane Armlets and Gauntlets, Wooden Masks, Lime Knives, Ornamental Shields, Neck and Breast Ornaments made of boar's tusks, Head Dresses made from feathers, Wooden Idols, Lime Gourds, Bark Beaters, Necklaces made of shell, Mouth Ornaments, Shell Armlets, Food Baskets, Feather Head Dresses, Bone Daggers, Water Buckets made from the palm wood, Bark Waist Belts, Flint Drills, Wooden Food Plates, &c.

In Case No. 18 there are Fishing Hooks, Fish Spears, Traps and Pots, Landing Nets, Pig Catchers, Arrow for shooting pigs, Fish Bags, Man Catcher made of cane with a spike to penetrate the back of the neck.

In Case No. 19 are Bows and Arrows, and Arm Gauntlets made of cane and palm wood, Paddles, &c.

On the wall above the stairs are some grotesque Masks, and on the wall at the northern end of the room is a large Grass Dress worn by a chief, and suspended from the ceiling are Canoes.

In table Cases Nos. 31 and 32 are Stone Axe Blades, Chinham Boxes made of carved bamboo, others covered with net work, and oblong Calabashes or Gourds used for Chinham. Chinham is a compound of lime and betel nut, and is used for chewing.

In table Cases Nos. 31 and 32 are Fan or Mouth Pipes made from small bamboo, long fine Combs, Nose Ornaments, some very long and straight, others curved at the end, Scent Bags, a fine stone Axe showing small fossil shells, a number of Slings used for throwing stones, Cocoa-nut Scrapers made of pinna shell, one end covered with gum and clay to form a handle.

Hanging from the gallery, and on the balustrade, are a number of Dresses, and on the walls over the cases are heavy Spears. Canoes are suspended from the ceiling.

GERMAN NEW GUINEA is represented by specimens in Table Cases Nos. 33 and 34, viz., Neck Ornaments with boars' tusks ornamented with small black and red seeds, Waist Belts, Armlets and Bracelets ornamented with small shells, Combs, Necklaces made of Dogs' Teeth, Net Bags, and Bags ornamented with seeds and shells, carved tortoise shell Gauntlet.

THE AUSTRALIAN ABORIGINAL specimens are exhibited in wall Cases Nos. 20 to 22 and table Cases Nos. 23 and 24.

In the wall Cases are Boomerangs, Nulla-nullas, Swords, Stone Axes in handles, Fire Sticks, Skin Water Bags, Shields, Heilimans, Dilly Bags, Emu Decoy made from a hollow piece of wood with a small hole left in the end to blow through, Womeras, Mills for grinding seeds for food, &c.

Table Cases Nos. 23 and 24 contain Stone Axe-heads, and Stone Mills used by the Aborigines. A window at top of stairs is decorated with Aboriginal Fishing and Fighting Spears.

Table Case No. 35 contains Implements used by the natives of the Darling River Districts in the manufacture of weapons, &c.

In the same case are two remarkable Wax Figures made by the Aboriginals of North Australia.

In wall Case No. 10 on ground floor are exhibited some Aboriginal and other "Mummies," viz.:—Head of a Mummy Child from Quito, Peru. Ancient Egyptian Cat. Body of Man from Sassafras, N.S.W. Woman and Child from Cairns, Queensland. Dried Body of a Child, 6 years old, from Goldie River, New Guinea.

THE NEW ZEALAND Ethnological Specimens are in table Cases Nos. 26 to 29.

In Case No. 26 there are casts of Flax Beaters and Fern Beaters, an oval-shaped carved Baton, a four-sided carved Baton, a flat Baton, a curved and carved Meri, a large Meri, Net Sinkers and Adzes.

In Cases Nos. 27 to 29 are ancient Maori Axes and Adzes, Greenstone Axes and Meris, Mens' Needles and Eardrops of jade or greenstone, Tikis, Meri made from the jawbone of the sperm whale.

MISCELLANEOUS COLLECTION—For comparison with the Australian, New Zealand and Island specimens the following from other countries are exhibited in Table Cases.

From Peru, Yucutan, Mexico and California a number of Implements and Utensils are exhibited in Case No. 36.

From India and Siam there are Palm Leaf Letters, Malay Sandals, &c., in Case No. 35.

From Egypt there are Mummy Cloths, Gold Earrings, Bronze Ornaments, &c., in Case No. 35.

European Prehistoric Stone and Flint Implements are in Case No. 25.

Some Miscellaneous specimens are in Case No. 37, such as Old Scottish Sword, German Needle-gun Bullets, French Chassepot and Mittrailleuse Bullets, Old English Spurs, Knives, Spoons, Keys, and Horseshoes, Roman Bronze Sword, Flint Lock of Old English Gun, Bolt and Nut from the old Top Rail of the Eddystone Lighthouse 1750.

From the Hawaiian Islands a fine piece of Tappa Cloth is exhibited in Case No. 34, and in the same Case is some Human Hair from one of the South Sea Islands, and specimens of Native Cloth obtained by Captain Cook in 1770 at the Sandwich Islands, and at Tahiti and Tonga.

A Collection of Flints and Tools representing the manufacture of Gun Flints is in Case No. 38. This is a nearly extinct industry, but is interesting as being the nearest approach, in modern times, to what must have been formerly a common occupation.

A COLLECTION OF STONE IMPLEMENTS is in the gallery in Table Cases. Although already noticed under their respective localities it may be interesting to many visitors to inspect these again collectively.

The Australian Aboriginal Implements are in Cases Nos. 23 and 24. These are of a very simple character. Some valuable and handsome examples of Stone work by the Maoris of New Zealand are in Cases Nos. 26 to 29. In Case No. 30 are specimens from the Islands of the Pacific. Including Stone Axe Heads from the Solomon Islands and New Britain, and a stalactite Pestle from the Marshall Islands. In Case No. 23 will be observed a little pile of Flint Flakes, which have been chipped off during the process of manufacture of some of the Implements, and in connection with this another glance at the collection illustrating the Gun Flint Industry, in Case No. 38, will be instructive.

After having inspected the Ethnological Collections in the Museum, it may be of interest to spend a few minutes over the collections of Relics, Medals, and other interesting exhibits in table Cases Nos. 17, 18 and 19, on the ground floor. A list of most of these will be found in the cases, but the most interesting to Australians are—

Compass of the ship "Endeavour" on her first voyage round the world. This Compass was preserved by Sir Joseph Banks, Naturalist of the "Endeavour," in his private museum at 32 Soho Square, London, and at his death passed into the hands of Dr. Brown, President of the Linnean Society, who was at one time private Secretary, or Librarian, to Sir Joseph Banks. It was sold at auction by his executors to Dr. Prince, of Crowborough, from whom it passed in to the possession of Mr. Thomas Toon, and was purchased by the Hon. Sir Saul Samuel, Agent-General for New South Wales, by whom it was sent to Sydney.

Two Collecting Jars used by the Naturalists who acccompanied Captain Cook. One of these was discovered in Sir Joseph Banks's old house. It was called " Captain Cook's Grog Flask," and had a label in Sir Joseph Banks's handwriting saying that it belonged to the great navigator.

Telescope belonging to Admiral Kemp, at one time a Midshipman under Captain Cook.

Glass Star presented by Captain Cook to the King of Aitataki Island.

Some Documents and Relics which belonged to the explorer, Dr. L. Leichhardt.

F, Cunninghame & Co., Printers, 146 Pitt-street, Sydney.